HER SHIFTER BABE

PERFECT PAIRS
BOOK SIX

AMELIA SHAW

CHAPTER 1
STACEY

There was no way I wouldn't be able to find Tommy in a town *this* small, right? I glanced around at the single street of shops. For a tiny country town, it sure was bustling with people. The whole area resounded with the noise of people rushing about, sitting and chatting in cafés over coffee while the typically mouth-watering aroma of barbecue hung thick and heavy in the air.

I gulped at the bile that rose instantly in my throat and sighed. I used to *love* barbecue, but presently I hated the smell of cooked meat. Even after all these months of pregnancy, I still hadn't been able to shake that part of my nausea. It really affected me, and I looked forward to the day it passed and my stomach settled back into its normal appetite.

My baby twisted and kicked inside my belly reminding me of their presence and making me smile despite the sadness filling my heart. "It's okay, bubba. We're almost there. I know it." Or so I hoped, anyway. I wasn't truly sure how much more time I had left, and I was just about run out of money. If I didn't find my

1

baby's father soon, I would be in some serious trouble. And so would the precious little life growing inside me.

I took a step toward a park bench as a wave of exhaustion passed over me. Darkness encroached on my vision, and I had to swallow against the heat that prickled up my neck.

"Hey!" a woman called out to me. "Are you okay?"

I instinctively gripped my belly and staggered forward, desperately needing to sit down and take a load off my feet.

The woman grabbed my arm and helped me to the bench seat only a few more steps away. "Sit, you poor thing. What's going on?"

I shook my hair a little, trying to garner some relief from the heat. I panted for breath and leaned forward, trying to get comfortable as my eyesight continued to swim. This poor woman had stopped for me, and although I was grateful, she really shouldn't have. The last thing I wanted was to be a bother to anyone. "I'm sorry," I managed. "You were going somewhere." I closed my eyes and forced myself to breathe, to draw in big, steady breaths. I couldn't faint. It would be too dangerous and far too expensive if they took me to the hospital. There was no way I could afford it.

The woman squeezed my arm. "Never you mind about that. I'll just throw these in the car and I'll be right back. Don't stress."

I forced myself to open my eyes and leaned back against the park bench. Goodness, it was hot. I'd heard that heat could make pregnancy extra uncomfortable, but this was ridiculous.

"Here," she said and opened a fresh bottle of water before handing it to me. "I'm Nancy. I don't think we've met before."

Gratitude for this kind stranger washed over me, and I thankfully took the water and gulped it down with relish. The cold was *so* refreshing on my poor throat, but I tried not to drink too fast, otherwise I knew I'd make myself sick. Some days I could barely even keep it down.

What did she say? Oh, yeah...

"I'm not from around here," I explained. "I'm Stacey."

"Stacey," she repeated. "Me either, at least originally. My bike broke down while I was driving through town, and I just never left."

I took another few sips of water then smiled up at Nancy, my savior of the day. "Thank you for that."

I expected Nancy to say goodbye and leave at that point, but she didn't go. Instead, she glanced from the big new car, to me, then back at the car again. She was a very pretty woman, with dark hair and a larger, curvy body that I personally admired. I'd been curvier, myself before falling pregnant, but months of not being able to eat without brutal sickness had taken a visible toll on my body.

Finally, Nancy turned toward me. "Hey, can I give you a lift somewhere? Or call someone for you? Something? Anything? I don't feel right about leaving you like this."

I unhooked the backpack from my shoulders and eased it around my body, holding my meagre possessions close. "Thanks. I, ah... I'm looking for someone, actually. A man."

She crossed her arms over her ample breasts and grinned at me. "Well, lucky for you, I happen to know a lot of the guys in this town."

I grimaced at her, a little surprised that she would boast about such a thing.

Nancy stared at me, then burst out laughing. "Oh, God! Not like that. My partners—I mean partner÷—has a lot of cousins in town. So, I can probably point you in the right direction, at least."

Partners? Did she mean business partners?

I licked my dry lips and forced myself unsteadily to my feet. How did I politely tell her that I was fine when I clearly wasn't. But I needed to continue my search, and Nancy was a complete stranger. And despite her kindness, I had no idea if I could trust her. We'd only just met, after all. How trusting could I really afford to be when my baby was relying on my instincts to keep him or her safe?

"How far along are you?" she asked gently when I didn't respond.

I pressed my hands to my belly, defensive of the question. But I shouldn't have been surprised that she was enquiring about my pregnancy. It's not like I could hide it any longer. "Um... I'm about six months, I think." I hadn't been to a doctor yet for date confirmation, and I'd read that pregnancies were usually counted in weeks, not months.

But who knows? This is my first, and what I know could be written on a pinhead!

Nancy tilted her head to the side like I was an exhibit she was studying. "So, who was it that you are looking for?"

"Um...," I began as I swallowed my anxiety. "His name is Tommy and he's tall," I said, lifting my arm to indicate his height roughly. "I think he might be around six feet two, maybe. And he's got blondish hair."

"Yeah, I know Tommy," she said.

My stomach swooped with nerves and my eyes widened.

Could my search really be over just like this?

Then Nancy grinned at me. "And how do you know him?"

Oh, God. I've never actually said the words out loud...

I gripped my belly for comfort, as though I could shield my child from the world by pure force of will. "Well..."

Nancy's jaw dropped as she gaped at me in shock. "Oh my God! Stacey, is Tommy the father?" she asked. "Does he know?"

I completely understood. And the truth was I didn't know a whole lot about Tommy realistically, but he had seemed like a truly decent guy when we'd been together. I could only hope that my instincts would be proven right. I pressed my lips together, almost not wanting to answer her. But I was way too fatigued to think of a good enough lie. "Oh, ah…" I let my words die on my tongue and dropped my gaze to my feet.

"How did you get here?" Nancy asked, not allowing me the alone time to devise a way to get out of here.

"The bus," I said, holding tightly to my backpack. Everything I owned in the whole world was in this silly little bag. I glanced across to the local diner.

Maybe I should get myself something to eat before finding Tommy. And I really need a shower. Maybe there's a cheap motel around here somewhere?

But before I could ask Nancy, she held out her hand. "Come on, Stacey. I've got a housewarming party to put on, and you're coming home with me."

I shook my head, biting down on my lower lip. "Oh, no. I can't inconvenience you like that." That wouldn't be fair to her at all. I was a hot mess. She didn't need me disrupting the rhythm of her new house.

Nancy grabbed my elbow and started tugging me toward her big car. "Tommy will be at the party this afternoon," she assured me. "I have no idea where he is now, but I know where he'll be in a few hours. So, come along. You can shower and eat and rest where it's cool. I promise you, you're safe with me."

In the next few moments, we were next to her humongous vehicle and I just stared at the woman in front of me.

Is this a guardian angel in human form?

My eyes burned, and I blinked quickly to dispel the tears. How could she possibly know what I needed? And what on earth was I going to do when I was finally face to face with Tommy once more?

Nancy's hand on my arm was gentle but insistent, so when she opened the car door, I clambered carefully inside. "This is nice." I said, unable to stop myself as I reached out to caress the shiny dashboard. I couldn't even imagine having a car like this.

"Yeah, it's new," she said. "I'm pregnant too actually, but only ten weeks, so no one really knows just yet."

"Oh, congratulations!" I gushed, happy for her even though we'd only just met. "Your husband must be so happy."

She laughed as though what I'd said was a major joke. "Yeah, you could say that. Let's get home and you can meet them."

"Them?" I repeated the word with a squeak.

But Nancy didn't answer, she simply offered me a smile as she drove.

What sort of crazy town have I found myself in?

We'd only driven for about three minutes when Nancy pulled the truck up outside a huge, old house.

"Wow, I love those windows," I said, entranced by the period features of the grand home. "You must have put a lot of work into it?"

"Oh, yeah. Heaps," she gushed. "It was a real mess when we took it on." Stacey hopped out of the car and opened the trunk, pulling out a few boxes.

I slipped out of the vehicle as well, my pulse already racing. Tommy wasn't here yet, but even so, I was *so* close to finally finding him. I could scarcely believe it.

This is really happening. It's like Fate has intervened.

"Let me help you," I said, popping on my backpack and grabbing one of the boxes from her.

"Oh, thanks," she said, picking up a shopping bag. "I appreciate that. These are just some last-minute things. Come on, let's get you settled."

I followed Nancy up the sidewalk to the house, noting the freshly planted flowers and the neat paving stones.

She forged ahead like the queen of her own queendom, opening the front door and bustling inside.

I gripped the box I held tightly with two hands and slowly crept inside, my anxiety in overdrive.

Her home was truly beautiful and seriously enormous. The floorboards shone with new lacquer and the high ceilings were decorated with pretty cornices and custom paint colors. I really appreciated the restoration, and I would know a good one when I saw it. I'd studied historic architecture and design before marrying a man way too old for me. I sighed at the memory.

"Just put that box down there," Nancy said, pointing to a small table in the entranceway.

I did what she said immediately, feeling unclean and unworthy of being in this beautiful house.

Nancy just grinned at me, then took off up the staircase. "Follow me. Just mind your step."

And so I did, running my hand over the solid wood balustrade, all the way up to the landing and along the hallway.

"This place is really... *wow*," I breathed.

"I'm glad you like it," Nancy said with genuine warmth before she pushed open a door. "This is a guest bedroom, and it has a shared bathroom with the bedroom next door, which I think is kind of cool."

I nodded. "Jack and Jill bathrooms?"

She shrugged. "If that's what you call it? Either way, these rooms will be perfect for my kids when they grow up. But for now, it's all yours," Nancy said as swept her arm out to invite me into the room.

I wandered inside, my feet and back aching from climbing the stairs. "Oh, now this is nice! I love the color palette you've chosen."

Soft pinks, grays, and warm eggshell-white tones met my eyes, relaxing me immediately. The room was large, with a queen bed in the center as well as a small seating area covered in soft, textured pillows. I couldn't help but run my fingers over the tendrils that featured on the woodwork.

"You seem well versed in design," Nancy said, curiosity evident in her tone.

I shrugged off my backpack and sighed as I slid my sore feet out of my tennis shoes, the soft carpet cushioning my toes as they got some air. "I have a degree in design," I explained. "I just haven't had the opportunity to use it much."

Nancy opened her mouth to say something else, probably to ask me a question, but a man's voice called out to her, and she sighed. "I've got to run. The bathroom's just through that door and there are plenty of towels and toiletries, so please help yourself!" She hurried back to the entrance, then called over her shoulder. "The party's not for another two hours, so if you want a nap, go for it."

"Thank you!" I called out, grateful beyond belief for this amazing woman.

"No problem at all," Nancy answered as she closed the door behind her, leaving me in a beautiful room in a stunning period home, just mere hours away from seeing Tommy again.

I waddled over to the luxurious, renovated white bathroom and held back the tears that swam furiously in my eyes. I wasn't sure how it had happened, but I was safe, and soon I'd be clean and well rested. I couldn't have even dared dream that everything would fall into place the way it just had for me. It was beyond wonderful.

This is the best day I've had in a very, very long time.

CHAPTER 2
TOMMY

"This house is amazing!" I called into my cousin's new home, knocking on the already open front door. "Hello?"

"Come in, Doc," Wade offered, striding toward me.

I stood on the threshold and held out the expensive bottle of whiskey I'd picked up on the way. "Happy housewarming, cousin. This place looks epic."

"Thanks," he said, taking the bottle and whistling at it. "Very nice. Thanks. Do you want the tour?"

"Sure." I followed my cousin into the huge kitchen and marveled at the open space. The cabinetry was all new and the floor-to-ceiling windows looked out onto the expansive back-yard and large, polished deck. "This is incredible, Wade. You guys have done so well restoring this place. It looks better than new."

Wade and Tanner had bought the historic mansion on the edge of town the moment their mate, Nancy, had taken a liking to it. Most of our family had originally felt it should be torn down rather than be restored, but my cousin's mate had been adamant about saving it and returning it to its former glory.

"Thanks," Wade said with a grin. "We put a fair amount of blood and sweat into the place. But come and check out the pergola Tanner and I just built. Mom and Dad are out in the yard already."

"Great," I said, still looking around in awe. "I've love to." This house had been a wreck for so long, it was hard to reconcile this incredible home with the sad and derelict dumpster fire it had been before.

"Is David coming too?" Wade asked as he grabbed a couple of beers from the ice bucket and handed one to me.

I twisted the top off and took a deep slug. "Yeah, he's coming. He just had to close the restaurant first."

My brother, David owned a steak place in town and was a *bit* of a control freak when it came to his proverbial baby, so he often did late hours. He opened most days and worked six days a week unless we had a family event on. As it was, he was closing early for the housewarming party today.

"Cool. Let's go outside."

I walked out the open patio doors and into the sunshine with my cold beer, admiring Wade's handiwork. "You know… our place could use a pergola as well."

David and I owned a new house closer to town, but we weren't handy like these guys. Not by a long shot.

Tanner walked over to us with a grin. "Well, if we ever finish this place and get back to work, you'll be our first call," he promised.

I reached out and shook my cousin's hand. I'd be happy to hire them and pay them what they were worth. Their work was quality with a capital Q. "Sounds like a plan," I replied.

Nancy came rushing up. "Tommy! Hey! I've been waiting for you to get here."

I leaned forward and kissed my cousin's mate on the cheek politely. "It's good to see you, Nancy. Your house is beautiful." I hadn't seen too much of the inside just yet, but I had to assume that they'd done as good a job on the bedrooms and bathrooms as they'd done on the kitchen. The whole mansion probably looked like a historic bed and breakfast.

"Thanks, I appreciate that. Is David here yet?" She glanced around.

A strange sense of concern began to creep into my heart at her line of questioning though it was entirely innocent enough. "No. Not yet. Why? What's wrong?"

She smiled at me, the mixture of emotions that flitted across her face an odd combination. Nancy was trying not to laugh, that much was obvious. She was also very amused, but there was a worry in her eyes I hadn't seen for a long time.

I dropped my voice to a whisper. "You're not spotting or having any health concerns, are you?" I asked, my brow furrowing. I was one of the only people who knew of Nancy's pregnancy, and it wasn't uncommon to miscarry, especially before twelve weeks.

She shook her head adamantly, allaying my fears instantly. "No. I'm good. Well, I feel like crap, actually, but that's a good sign according to my mother-in-law."

Relief washed over me at her upbeat response. "Then what's the matter? I can tell something's up with you."

Nancy wrung her hands and bit her lower lip. "I met someone in town today and invited her along to the party."

I waited, wondering when this was going to become relevant to me. "Yes?" I prompted.

"Her name's Stacey," Nancy went on. "And she's been tirelessly looking all over the state for you."

The bottom fell out of my stomach at the mention of the girl's name that I'd spent just one glorious night with about six months ago. "Ah... Stacey, you say?" I shifted my feet and moved my beer from one hand to the other.

It can't possibly be the same woman.

"Yeah. Beautiful blonde... long hair," Nancy answered.

"Curvy, like you?" I asked hesitantly.

Nancy's lips pressed into a thin line. "No. She's quite thin, overall."

I relaxed a little, able to breathe again. "Then it couldn't have been the Stacey I was thinking of."

The woman I'd spent a night of unbridled passion with while on a conference in the city had curves for days. She'd possessed the most luscious breasts, and she'd wrapped her deliciously thick thighs around me in a way that had made me believe in Heaven.

Nancy's eyebrows shot up. "Um, I'm pretty sure it's the one you're thinking of. Can you just come inside and meet her? She's a bit nervous. Like I said, she's come a long way."

Wade and Tanner regarded me with a knowing expression.

I swallowed the lump in my throat and nodded. "Ah, yeah... sure," I agreed. What else could I say?

"Come on," Nancy said, hustling back toward the house.

I gave my cousins a guilty smile and headed off after their mate. When I'd met Stacey, our chemistry had been electric and unlike anything I'd ever felt for anyone else. But she'd disappeared at the end of the night, and I'd never had the chance to see her again.

We walked through the kitchen, past the front door and into a small adjacent sitting room with a large L-shaped couch and a wall of colorful books.

Waiting by the door on the other side of the cozy room was Stacey. She had a pair of jeans on and a long, baggy sweater. Her face was pale, and she was definitely much thinner than I remembered. She looked like she'd lost twenty pounds, maybe more.

"Stacey!" I said with a welcoming smile. "It's so nice to see you again. How are you?" I took a step toward her.

The young woman's lips quivered as her hands came up to grip her belly protectively—her very round, *very* pregnant belly.

I stopped mid-stride.

Oh, my God.

"Ah..." I scarcely managed as my breath caught in my throat.

"Yes, I'm pregnant," Stacey confirmed. "And yes, it's yours. I've been looking everywhere for you. You haven't been the easiest man to find."

My jaw dropped, and I rocked back on my heels. "Oh... wow."

Stacey stared at me, her big blue eyes wide and afraid. "I couldn't find you."

"I'm so sorry," I said, remembering our encounter now with less than rosy glasses. "I had the same issue. You were gone by the next morning, and I didn't have your full name, or a number to contact you." My pride had been the only thing that had prevented me from sending a private investigator after her. If she didn't want to see me again after the incredible night we'd shared, I didn't want to be the one to force her.

"Yeah... that was my fault. I shouldn't have left like that," she said quietly, her cheeks flushing with shame.

I immediately wanted to rush over and comfort her, but I had no idea if that was what she wanted. "So..." I said, calculating dates in my mind. "You'd be... about twenty-six weeks along now, give or take?"

I'm going to be a father. I can't believe it.

Part of me still reeled with shock, sitting on a chair in the corner of my mind unable to speak. It was a lot to take in so suddenly and without warning.

She shrugged, her lips downturned in a grimace. "I don't know. I haven't been able to see a doctor yet."

My jaw dropped. "Oh..."

Damn it!

If I'd known she was pregnant, she would have received the best of care. But instead, she'd been all alone, searching the damn country for me. "Well, we can go right now if you want. I'll do the ultrasound myself." I needed to get her booked in with an OB-GYN as soon as possible. I had a friend from college that practiced in town and was only about twenty minutes away.

She looked as pale as the off-white walls of the study. She was probably anemic and needed bloodwork done. And from the looks of her, she was struggling to keep anything down, which wasn't ideal for her or our baby.

"Thank you, I'd like that, but maybe not today. I think I need to rest a little longer. I've been on the road a long time." Her small, determined smile hit me in the stomach like an anvil to the head in old cartoons, hard and low, stealing my breath away.

Nancy coughed, clearing her throat. "Okay, well I might go and get Stacey something to eat... but Tommy?"

I dragged my gaze away from the beautiful woman carrying my child, to my cousin's mate. "Yeah?"

"Has she met David yet?"

Oh... shiiiitt...

"Who's David?" Stacey asked, her forehead crinkling with confusion from the other side of the room. "I don't know anyone by that name."

I swallowed hard. "Thanks, Nancy."

She nodded and headed for the door, shutting it behind her as she went to offer us some privacy.

When I turned back around to Stacey, she'd moved to the couch and was sitting on the edge, with a hand pressed into her lower back. "She's so nice," she offered. "I can't believe my luck in running into her and then her being able to bring me straight to you after all this time."

I nodded and gulped, not even sure what to say next. How

the hell was I going to explain to her that my brother and I were a perfect pair, designed for the love of one woman? What would that mean for our future together? And what was David going to do when he found out about Stacey and her present situation?

"Yeah, Nancy is amazing," I agreed, walking over to the window to stare out at the street.

My brother would be arriving soon.

What am I going to do?

"I'm sorry to just... surprise you like this," Stacey said. "I never meant for this to happen, and then I didn't have anywhere else to go," she trailed off.

I turned around and gaped at her. "Never apologize for finding me, Stacey. I only wish you'd come to me as soon as you found out you were pregnant."

She rubbed her belly in a circular motion. "Yeah... again, I'm sorry. I wasn't exactly in the best place when we met, then I had to get my life on track, only for the pregnancy to kind of derail everything."

"I'm sorry," I said, feeling my heart squeeze tight with regret. "I would have helped you if I'd known."

David and I had an older sister, so we knew firsthand how difficult pregnancy could be, and how unforgiving some employers were when it came the unexpected miracle of life.

"I know," she said with a sigh. "I'm just so glad I found you."

I didn't ask her how she'd managed to track me down this far on her own. All she'd had from that fateful night was my first name and the knowledge that I was a doctor.

Perhaps that was enough?

I shoved my hands into my pockets to stop myself from reaching out for her. Even though she looked exhausted and had lost weight, she was still incredibly beautiful, and I didn't want to overstep boundaries. She'd come to me for support, to get help for our child. That didn't necessarily mean she wanted to be immediately thrust into a relationship again.

"Hey, what was Nancy saying before, about a David. Who's that?"

I inhaled sharply and ignored my cell phone as it rang in my pocket. "He's my brother. Fraternal twin, actually."

Stacey's eyes widened at the sudden realization of what that truth could potentially mean. "Oh my God! You're a twin? I hope I don't have more than one in here." She rubbed her belly quickly, her stress showing.

I went to open my mouth and tell her that fraternal twins came from the mother's line, then stopped myself. Perfect pairs weren't normal, so my spouting off some rubbish that I'd tell another patient wasn't right in this instance. Instead, I forced a smile. "You look the right size for a single baby, but we'll do an ultrasound as soon as possible, just to make sure."

She nodded and smiled at me, still clutching her belly, which caused my heart swell with a deep and natural sense of pride and the intrinsic desire to protect her at all costs. "So, you two are close, then? David and you?"

I nodded, feeling my anxiety rise, so I began pacing the study in front of the window. "Yes, we live together, actually. He runs a restaurant in town, so he's barely home, but he's a really good guy. I think you'll like him."

Stacey smiling politely.

Meanwhile, my stomach twisted with worry. How was I going to tell her the truth about David and me, and that she was the mate we were meant to share?

CHAPTER 3

DAVID

I sighed. My brother wasn't picking up the phone, but it didn't really matter now. I was already running late, but at least I had the cake I'd promised Nancy I would bring and was on my way there now.

I slid the cake box carefully onto the car seat next to me and shut the door. I hadn't closed the restaurant early on a Saturday in a long time, but I didn't have a manager I trusted enough to run the evening shift at the moment, so there wasn't much choice in the matter. In fact, if I were being honest, I was actually looking forward to a relaxed afternoon and a few beers with my extended family.

Hopefully, the housewarming party would stretch into the evening like so many of our family events did, but if it didn't... Tommy and I could head out to dinner or have an early night.

God knows I need one!

I'd been going too hard for too long, and so had Tommy. We always said to one another we'd work our butts off until our mate showed up in our lives, then we could slow down, just like Wade and Tanner had. Unfortunately, we were over forty now, and the woman who was meant to complete us was still nothing more than a figment of our collective imaginations.

It took me less than five minutes to pull up outside Tanner, Wade, and Nancy's new place. The street was literally lined with cars from one end to the other, and the aroma of barbecue filled the neighborhood. I made an appreciative noise in my throat, grabbed the cake box and headed inside. They'd done a great job on the façade, and the gardens were planted and landscaped as well.

I admired their restoration and attitude toward maintaining its original integrity, but I certainly couldn't imagine doing gardening like that myself. Though gorgeous, the colorful, cottage-style gardens were no doubt hugely labor-intensive and digging in the dirt really wasn't my thing. I had my hands full with a restaurant, which ran me off my feet as it was.

I knocked on the door and plastered a smile on my face.

Nancy was there moments later, a plate of food in hand. "Oh! David. You made it."

"Hey, Nancy," I said, greeting her with a kiss on the cheek. "Where do you want me to put the cake?"

"Oh, on the kitchen counter please. I'm really excited about this."

I grinned at her. The cake wasn't *just* an ordinary cake, it was a gender reveal as well. Nancy had some bloodwork done early last week, and my brother had rushed through the results to find out the gender of the baby for her. Both my pastry chef and I knew the results, but no one else. "Right. I'll go take it in for you." I took my leave of Nancy and found Wade standing in the kitchen with a beer.

"Hey, cousin," I said. "Congratulations on the house and the... you know." I winked, the unspoken reference to his soon to be baby bundle.

Wade grinned at me. "Yeah... you too, I guess."

I slid the cake box further away from the edge of the counter, not wanting it to fall and smash. That had taken far too many hours of baking and decorating to have it destroyed. "Me too?" I asked, grimacing at my cousin in confusion. I didn't have a new house, a mate, or a baby on the way.

What is he talking about?

"Yeah... Stacey and the..." Wade made a belly-rubbing gesture.

It made no sense to me whatsoever. "Huh?"

Wade glanced back at the front door, his expression suddenly one of a man who'd just put his foot in it. "Ah... I thought... I mean, sorry, mate. You need to go talk to Tommy."

My gut tightened with unease, and a shiver raced up my spine, but I thanked my cousin awkwardly and headed in the direction I'd seen Nancy wander off to. There was another door just off the foyer, and I knocked on it, wanting to know what the hell was going on. The door swung inward, and Nancy was there. "Hey, Nancy," I said. "Have you seen my brother?"

Nancy inhaled sharply, as though she were carrying the weight of the world on her shoulders and my presence had disrupted her balance. "Yeah, he's in here," she said. Nancy stepped back and the scene before me unraveled like a bad sitcom.

There was my brother, sitting on a L-shaped sofa next to a beautiful young woman. I was immediately struck by the curve of her cheek and the glistening health of her long blonde hair.

Tommy stood up, turning toward me, and held out his hand to the woman to help her up.

She took his offered hand and stood awkwardly.

And it was only when she got to her feet and her baggy cardigan fell open that I understood why her movement was labored. My eyes widened upon drinking in her huge, pregnant belly. A strangled gasp stuck in my throat as my heart began to race, but I licked my lips and stepped forward, inexplicably determined to introduce myself. "Hello," I managed to say, walking further into the room. "I'm David."

"Hi, David," the beautiful woman answered, a bright smile lighting up her otherwise fatigue-plagued features. "I'm Stacey."

I stood facing them together, noting the way my brother remained by her side. He wasn't touching her, but I could feel the protectiveness he felt toward her even from where I stood.

"Hi, Stacey," I ventured, my world slipping sideways like I was taking a tumble across a ship's deck at sea.

Nancy slipped out of the room and shut the door quietly behind her, suspiciously leaving the three of us alone.

"How are you feeling?" I asked as I nodded at her swollen belly.

She gripped the sides of her precious bundle, accentuating the round bump even more, and making her seem perfect. "Really tired," she admitted. "And still a bit nauseous, if I'm honest."

"Always be honest," I said immediately, sounding a little firmer than I had meant to. "I mean... there's no point in covering up the truth, right?" I preferred people who were forthright and truthful. I always had.

Stacey nodded in agreement. "Right."

I lifted my gaze to my brother, trying to keep the accusation out of my gaze. It was potentially possible—although unlikely— that Stacey was *just* a patient of his, but there was something about the tension in the room that was telling me there was, in fact, a lot more going on right under my nose than I was aware of... and I had to know. My insides twisted as I grounded myself as best I could for what was coming. "Tommy?"

My brother straightened and tensed as though preparing himself to deliver horrible news. "I met Stacey when I was in the city six months ago, and we slept together."

My gut twisted again, this time much more violently.

Fuck...

I knew without asking what was coming next, but I had to hear it said. This wasn't the sort of thing you made assumptions about. I needed to hear the truth. "So, this baby is yours?" I asked carefully.

My shifter howled inside my mind, enraged and heartbroken all at once as the question hung between us. I'd spent twenty-five years being inscrutably careful with every girlfriend I'd ever had, dutifully waiting for our mate to find us before bringing life into this world.

What the hell has my brother done?

Tommy made a pained sounding noise in his throat. "David..." he began.

I swallowed hard.

Maybe I don't need to hear it, after all.

I took a step away from them both, feeling shame and pain rain down upon me in unfathomable measures. My whole life up until this point had been a lie. Every plan my brother and I had ever made together was now obsolete. It was a farce. I'd wasted my youth on a dream! "Congratulations," I managed to say as I staggered back to the door I'd come through.

Poor Stacey looked distraught, though I wasn't quite sure why.

All I knew was that I couldn't bear to look at her. It hurt too much. And it wasn't her fault that my stupid brother had broken our ability to be a perfect pair-bonded family like we were always destined to be.

And I knew my brother well enough to know he'd be committed to Stacey and their baby, irrespective of whether or not they ended up together ultimately. But with her being so young and beautiful, not to mention the natural mother of his first child... why wouldn't he choose to be with her forever? And that left me resoundingly alone, my part in a Fated ménage finally dashed like waves upon jagged rocks.

"David, wait! Come back, please. I haven't explained yet. *Please.*"

I shook my head. I just couldn't. "No, brother." I was choking now, and I needed to get away. As far away as possible. "You have your path, it seems. And it's one you obviously need to walk alone."

"David, I'm sorry!" Stacey called out, her brow furrowed in confusion at my reaction. "I didn't mean to upset you with my news."

I offered a grim smile to the young woman who'd just turned my world upside down and inside out. "Welcome to the family, Stacey." Then I fell through the door and managed to slam it shut behind me. I didn't go and see Nancy or my cousins. I couldn't think, couldn't function. I couldn't be at a family event making small talk while trying to be happy for my cousins when I wasn't feeling anything other than a crushing sense of despair.

I jogged through the front door, unable to look back, slid into my car and took off home—the home I shared with Tommy.

Maybe I should move out? Let them have the house?

Tommy could buy me out, and I could get my own place. I'd never lived alone, but it was probably high time I started. After all, I'd have to find my own mate now, because my brother had clearly chosen his woman. That was for sure.

I soon arrived home, I could scarcely breathe. My chest felt too tight, and my wolf shifter was howling uncontrollably within me. I needed to shift and run, to mourn the future I'd worked so hard for—and now lost. Instead of getting out of the car, I turned the engine back on and reversed, driving back toward my parents' place. They lived on the edge of the forest and owned ten beautiful acres of untouched land.

More than enough room to be able to run while also staying

safe. As soon as I pulled up, I jumped out of the car and noticed the lights on. I didn't bother to check out who might have stopped by, I just ran around the house, letting myself into their yard before stripping off my jeans and shirt.

My wolf tore through me in record time, my skin transforming into fur as my shifter forced me to all fours, and a howl ripped from my throat. In my animal form, the pain was somehow less, more bearable, and the downward spiral of depressive emotions and thoughts I'd been drowning in ground to an unexpected halt.

In fact, in my wolf form, I could feel a blink of hope in the darkness of my human despair, of enjoying my brother's baby as a family. But I squashed the thought and impulse, upset at my wolf's baseless assumptions.

How can he think I would just become the third wheel in my brother's relationship?

I had *a lot* more pride than that. I deserved a woman who loved me too. One who chose me as well as Tommy. Or that had been the original plan, anyway.

I shook off the morose thoughts and let go of my humanity, my brain shifting fully into my baser wolf as I ran into the forest. My parents didn't even have a back fence built, their yard just extended back forever. So, I ran and ran, dodging the larger trees and jumping over low lying shrubs that threatened to ensnare me.

Adrenaline began to pound through my veins, and I pushed myself harder and faster, my heart hammering against my ribcage like a drum. Maybe I'd just continue running and never stop.

After all, what is there to go back for now?

My wolf howled, his voice echoing into the night and rising to greet the cold and distant moon.

CHAPTER 4
STACEY

I turned toward Tommy with tears clouding my vision. "What's going on, Tommy?" I gasped. "Why was he so upset about my pregnancy?"

Tommy and David live together... but why?

David's reaction to me and my baby bump had been tantamount to watching someone get their heart broken in a very obvious, very public way. His pain and shock had been palpable, which made no sense.

Who reacts that way to a woman's pregnancy?

Unless David wasn't a brother after all, but a lover? In which case his hurt would make a lot more sense.

Tommy ran a hand through his hair and collapsed onto the couch, his expression soured with a grimace. "Damn it. I really didn't want him finding out like that."

I moved over to the window and watched as David hurried to his expensive-looking car, jumped inside, and raced off.

Damn it, was right. David was incredibly gorgeous. If I was being blunt, he was too hot for my sanity, especially if my baby was going to be related to him. I'd thought Tommy was as handsome as men came, and he was. But David's raw sexuality poured off him like a waterfall.

How can they be gay?

My hormones were telling me it made *no* sense, so I had to find out. Now. The moment David was down the road and out of sight, I shivered with an unease I hadn't ever felt before. It was strange in a way I couldn't wrap my head around.

"Are you cold?" Tommy asked from behind me.

I shook my head as I turned back around. "No, I'm not. But you need to tell me what's going on with David." When he didn't respond straight away, I crossed my arms over my chest and sighed. "You can tell me the truth, Tommy. I'm an open-minded person, but I just need to know. Is David your... lover?"

The closeness and intimacy they shared together was obvious, but asking the question was still difficult for me. I prided myself on being an accepting individual, but it smarted a little, since it hadn't even occurred to me once that Tommy might be gay or bisexual. Married or divorced, maybe. But during the night we'd spent together, there hadn't been a single moment where I'd had cause to wonder about Tommy's sexuality.

"Oh, hell no!" Tommy jumped to his feet. "We're *brothers*. Literally. We're fraternal twins. I've got photos ... My parents will be here soon enough. You can ask them."

I nodded slowly, taking him at his word as I shook the tension out of my shoulders. "Then what was that all about? It seems a bit weird that your brother, who I've never met, would get so distraught over our baby."

"Ah... oh, fuck." Tommy paced the room. "I'm going to have to tell you the truth to explain this situation, but you're going to have to keep your mind open about it. Okay?"

"I can do that. But you're not bisexual or married, are you?"

Tommy shook his head. "No, that's not for me. I'm single and straight as the day is long."

"Okay." A rush of relief washed over me, but there was still a tension in my gut I couldn't resolve. He wasn't gay or bisexual and he wasn't married, so what else could it be? I honestly had no idea what he was going to say, but at least he'd answered my questions and been upfront so far.

I'll just have to see where this goes...

"In my family, twin boys are sometimes born in what is termed a 'perfect pair'. It means that David and I are kind of opposite of each other in every way. I'm not as serious and I'm much funnier, at least, according to the family. He's a fucking perfectionist, and way too smart for his own good. Even our coloring is different. I'm lighter and taller. He's darker and shorter. Our strengths and weaknesses basically complement each other."

I nodded as if an odd familial term for twins explained any of our current predicament. "Okay. So, what're are you trying to say, Tommy?"

He dragged in a huge breath, running another frazzled hand through his gorgeous blond hair. "Well, in our family, most perfect pairs end up married to one woman. They share a family like Wade and Tanner, Nancy's husbands."

"Nancy's... husbands?" I felt my eyes grow wide and my jaw hit the floor.

Tommy nodded slowly. "She didn't tell you about that yet?"

"Well... no. She failed to mention that."

Oh, shit. I've found myself in some kind of polygamous family cult. Crap. Not what I had in mind!

Tommy went on, oblivious to the fact I was beginning to hyperventilate.

"So, that's what David was upset about. We were always meant to find the right woman together. Love her together, be a complete family. And now, with you and I..." He sighed and sat down with a thump. "I hate this. I mean, I'm *so* happy for us, for you and me—please don't misunderstand. But my brother… we'd always planned our life to unfold a certain way… but I guess it doesn't matter now."

My head was starting to spin when there was a knock at the door.

Nancy stuck her head in, her voice soft. "Was that David I just saw driving off—" She paused mid-sentence, her gaze fixated on me. "Whoa, you need to sit down!" She rushed over to me, grabbed my hand, and gently encouraged me sit on the couch.

My stomach strained, feeling somehow tighter with my quick breathing. I was trying not to give in to hyperventilating completely, but that was fast becoming a problem. "Is it true?" I managed to get out in between breaths. "That you have two?"

Nancy frowned and glanced over at Tommy for some clarification or point of reference.

Tommy sighed again. "Sorry, Nancy. I had to tell her about perfect pair marriages after David kind of freaked out and took off."

Nancy chuckled softly and kneeled in front of me. "Just breathe, slowly. Or I'll get you a paper bag."

I closed my eyes and focused on wrangling my panic back under control. After a minute or two, when I could finally breathe more calmly, I opened my eyes again and met Nancy's gaze. I still wanted an answer. "Well?" I pressed, even though I had no real right to enquire about her personal life. She was family now, but realistically we'd only just met. She certainly didn't deserve my emotion-driven snappiness, but my pregnancy hormones were ramping up and making me feel more panicked and grumpier than usual.

Nancy didn't get upset at my tone of voice in the slightest. In fact, she took it in stride and instead she got to her feet with a grin. "I think you're going to fit right in around here, Stacey.

Come on, come along and meet my husbands. We're just about to cut the cake." Nancy dragged me to my feet and clung to my hand as she led me from the sitting room and into the rest of her beautiful house.

"I can't believe it," I whispered, mostly to myself, my mind reeling.

Nancy chuckled. "Yeah, I know, right? I freaked the hell out too. I remember it like it was just yesterday."

"You did?" I asked, looking toward the woman, who was glowing with good health and happiness.

"Yeah, of course!" She laughed. "I was on my bike, riding like a bat out of hell, looking for a safe place to hide from my asshole ex, when a couple of brothers up and decided they both wanted me! Ah... *nope.* It blew my mind, and I panicked *big* time. That wasn't the kind of life I'd dreamed of, or I ever thought I'd end up with."

The brothers she was talking about glided up and took her from my grasp, kissing her and whispering to her in a coordinated way that almost made their intimate interaction look like a dance.

Finally, she got them to stop petting her and she gestured to me. "Guys, this is the young lady I was telling you about, Stacey." She smiled broadly. "Stacey, this is Tanner and Wade, my husbands and mates."

I nodded at the two men who grinned at me.

"Welcome to our housewarming," the brother called Wade said. "Nancy says you'll be staying here for a while?"

"Ah..." My voice died in my throat.

"Yes, she is," Nancy said quickly, filling in for me. "She's already set up in the guest suite."

I managed to smile, though I didn't feel quite comfortable in agreeing to anything out loud just yet.

"Come on. Let's go cut that beautiful cake." Wade swept his

wife away, Tanner close behind, and I ended up watching from the dining area as they began the ritual of speeches and cake cutting. They thanked everyone present, then announced their pregnancy to one and all. The whole room lit up with happiness and cheers.

"Are you doing okay?" Tommy whispered to me, sliding up behind me.

"Yeah, I think so," I managed, even though I wasn't sure how I was. This entire situation seemed crazy. It defied everything I'd grown up to know as normal and socially acceptable. And yet as I watched Nancy and her men, I couldn't help but see them as nothing more than a beautiful family—just people who were committed to one another and in love.

"I have a role to play in the next part of the reveal," Tommy said into my ear, touching my lower back gently. "Excuse me. I'll be back."

"It's a boy!" The collective family all around us cried as the cake was cut and slices of brilliant blue cake were revealed.

Tommy walked over to the new throuple family and handed them a card.

"Thanks," Nancy said, but didn't move to open it.

"You'll want to open that now." Tommy gestured with a grin. "Because I didn't tell you *everything* we saw at the early scan."

Nancy's brow creased as she opened the envelope and pulled out the contents. A single ultrasound image. She stared at it for several long moments as silence descended upon the room. "Is that...?" She pointed at the picture, her eyes like saucers.

"I can't say for certain," Tommy announced, "but I'm pretty sure that you are carrying the next set of perfect pair boys in the family!"

"Oh my God!" Nancy cried, clasping her hands to her cheeks, gobsmacked as the room erupted with delighted laughter and riotous cheering once more.

Nancy was snatched up by her proud husbands, who kissed and hugged her like she was the queen of their world and just made them the happiest men on Earth.

Tommy walked back to me, his hands shoved into his pants pockets. "I've been holding onto that secret all week," he shared with me, a twinkle in his eye.

I smiled at him but wasn't sure how to process all the emotions coursing through me. This was *a lot* to take in on top of being six months pregnant. "I think I need to sit down," I said.

"Okay, no problem. Where do you want to go?" he asked.

"My room," I answered, not even thinking about it before the words spilled from my lips. "Would you mind grabbing me a soda, please?" My stomach liked the fizzy bubbles for some reason. They seemed to help whenever nausea struck.

Tommy grabbed a drink from one of the buckets of ice, and we headed upstairs.

I didn't know why he was following me, but we probably needed to talk more, I imagined. Thankfully, I'd made the bed again after my nap, so everything looked neat and tidy. I sat down on the floral comforter and took a steadying breath.

Tommy stood by the door, clearly not wanting to overstep the mark on my personal space. "Can I stay for a moment?" he asked.

"Sure," I said, gesturing to the armchair in the corner of the room. "It looks like Nancy is happy to allow me to stay here for a while, which is nice of her."

"It is," Tommy said, before passing me my soda and sitting down. "Can you tell me more about your situation, Stacey? I mean... I love that you came all this way to tell me about our baby face to face, but do you have to leave again at some point? Do you have family waiting, or anything to get back to?" he asked.

I shook my head, then took a sip of the refreshing beverage.

"No, nothing like that. My parents are elderly now and can't really help me. I was working on a casual basis, but as soon as my pregnancy became obvious, I was no longer needed."

I raised my gaze to meet his eyes and my anxiety came flooding back at what I had to admit next. "I was married," I stuttered, tripping over the words. "He wasn't very... nice to me, so I ran away. And that was the night I met you. I was hiding, looking for somewhere safe to stay for a while and wandered into the hotel to book a room."

Tommy chuckled. "And you literally ran into me in the foyer," he recalled.

I gulped and nodded my head. "You... you saved my life in a lot of ways that night, Tommy." I'd wanted to tell him so many times, so I paused to make sure I got it out right. "I'd managed to pack everything I needed in my car, but my ex is, well *was* very persistent about getting me back at the time, and I was afraid. But that night we spent together? You showed me what passion could be and what kindness was. I... could never go back after having experienced that. That's why I set out to find you."

Tommy stood up and moved over to my bed. He sat down next to me and put his arm around me, not speaking, just offering me his physical strength and silent comfort as my past haunted me.

I dropped my head onto his shoulder as if it was the most natural thing in the world and closed my eyes. It had been a very long, *very* tiring six months of travel and fear. But if I was lucky, if I could accept all this... "perfect pairs" business, it was beginning to look like I'd finally reached my destination.

My baby and I are finally safe.

TOMMY

Stacey fell asleep after some time of just resting on my shoulder—clearly exhausted emotionally as well as physically after everything she'd been through—so I eased her gently to down to the mattress and crept downstairs, leaving my very pregnant mate safe and sound in Nancy's guest suite.

The night I'd met Stacey I had been as drunk as I could be while remaining upright. I'd endured a boring-ass medical conference all day, and partaken in drinks at lunchtime, and again after the lectures had finished.

I'd managed to rustle some dinner up as well as more wine, and then stumbled my way through the lobby towards the elevators, wanting nothing more than to lie down and drink two gallons of water. But it seemed that Fate had other ideas, because I'd literally run into the most beautiful woman I'd ever seen—Stacey. With her gorgeous long blonde hair and bountiful curves, she would've made any hot-blooded male's mouth water.

When she'd grabbed my arm to steady herself in her rush through the lobby, there had been a strange, electric buzz that passed between us. It was enough to knock some of the alcohol out of my system and sober me up a little, but not enough to knock me off my feet.

In my tipsy, blasé state I'd dismissed the feeling initially, and we started chatting. She'd been looking to book a room, and I'd offered her my spare. I'd paid for a full suite, and the physician I'd planned to travel with had canceled on me at the last minute.

She'd seemed on edge but grateful for my offer of hospitality and came up with me to my suite. We'd shared wine and room service and chatted about nothing in particular. I remember being happy that she seemed more comfortable and relaxed, and then she kissed me, pulling me headlong into a vortex of pleasure unlike anything I'd ever known.

Looking back now, I should have realized she was special. But with the alcohol dulling my senses, and the absence of my twin, I'd dismissed any signs that indicated she was meant to be ours. But now, I was sure. The tingle in her touch was decreasing with each moment we were together, but she was meant to be mine. I was certain. The *zing* was only there to act as a lightning rod, to help a male recognize the bond. It wasn't supposed to last forever.

But how do I tell David?

And was it really possible that she was somehow my mate and not my twin's? Did perfect pairs ever marry different women? I didn't even know if that was possible or a thing. I certainly wasn't aware of any such instances.

With these questions and many more niggling at my mind, I made my way downstairs to find that most of the family had gone home. Nancy and my cousins, along with my aunt and uncle, however, were still sitting under the pergola enjoying chatter, drinks, and snacks together by the fire pit.

"Tommy!" Nancy called out, waving me over. "Come, sit!"

I fell into one of the outdoor chairs with a groan, my stomach lurching. "Damn. I think I forgot to eat."

"There's plenty of leftovers," Nancy offered, waving her hand at the laden table in front of us. "Help yourself."

I reached for a platter of sandwiches and pulled it toward me, picking one up that appeared to be filled with chicken salad. "Thanks."

"So," Wade said with a grin, "we hear the final perfect pair have found their woman."

My aunt and uncle sat up straighter in their chairs, their curiosity immediately piqued. "What do you mean?" they asked.

I chewed my sandwich then awkwardly shrugged. "Stacey is mine, I'm pretty sure. But I don't think she's David's mate."

"How is that possible?" Nancy gasped, glancing over at her in-laws. "Aren't perfect pairs meant to *always* share a woman?"

Aunt Tess picked up her glass of wine and held it in thought. "Well... not always. Some of our mountain lion cousins married separate women—" she began.

"But that didn't even work out!" Uncle Barry interjected. "They ended up finding their real mate later on."

"True," Aunt Tess acknowledged, nodding slowly.

I grabbed another sandwich and sat back in my chair. "So, you're telling me that either Stacey is David's mate too... or she's not mine to begin with, and I have to tell her that?"

Both options seemed strange and unpalatable, and my initial feelings were that I didn't want to deal with either. I wasn't sure how I'd feel about sharing Stacey, but I also didn't want to have to tell her that all she'd ever be to me was *just* the biological mother of my child because my real perfect pairs mate was still out there somewhere.

"How did David respond to her?" Nancy said, "I saw him run from the house, so I assume it wasn't good."

I chewed thoughtfully before answering. "Ah... no. Not good

at all. My brother took one look at Stacey's pregnant belly and then pretty much headed for the hills."

"So, he didn't touch her?" Tanner asked, one brow cocked in question.

I shook my head. "Nope. He didn't get that far. He just asked if the baby was mine, then bolted. He looked pretty shattered, to be honest. It was awful."

Tanner grinned. "Then you won't know until they make physical contact. David has to shake her hand or something. I'm sure he was just reacting out of shock."

"Didn't you keel over when you met Stacey?" Nancy asked me, sitting forward on her chair and reaching for a small plate that contained a piece of pie. "My boys did."

I chuckled softly, imagining her "boys" falling to their knees from the mere touch of their mate's hand. "Ah, not really. I mean... I felt an electrical buzz a bit. But I was *so* drunk when we met, like... blind drunk. So, I think that might have taken the edge off the whole 'knocking me to the ground part.'"

Tanner laughed. "Well, don't tell Markus and Oliver that, they'll be jealous as hell."

I glanced around, noting their absence. "Did they come today?"

"Oh, yeah," Nancy said. "But Lexie is *so* pregnant, she didn't want to stay long. She's really uncomfortable at the moment, poor thing."

I nodded absently. "Yeah, I saw her a few days ago." She was past her due date and getting grouchier by the day.

"So, what are you going to do about David?" Aunt Tess asked.

I grabbed a chicken leg from another platter in front of me and shrugged for the second time since sitting down. "I have no idea."

"Yes, you do," Nancy said, glaring at me like I was a fool. "You've got to get them together. It's the only way."

"Stacey's exhausted," I said, worry coursing through me unexpectedly. "I don't want to put any more on her today."

"Well, bring him tomorrow," Nancy resolved. "Stacey can stay here, and I'll do what I can to help her rest and recover from whatever she's been through, but it looks like it's been a lot."

The group looked at me expectantly, but I kept my lips firmly shut. I only knew a fraction of the trials and tribulations that Stacey had gone through to find me, and I wasn't about to blab that around my family without her consent. "That would be great," I said finally. "And I'll see what I can do to work on David."

"And get her in for that ultrasound," Nancy added, grinning at me. "You never know. Hers might show the same thing mine did."

I laughed, not sure which way I wanted the results of the ultrasound to go. "It's possible. But she's on the smaller side for thirty weeks, so I'd guess she only has one baby in there."

Nancy pouted. "Oh, no! I forgot about my belly. I'm going to be huge, aren't I?"

The rest of the family went on to tell her how beautiful she was and that she didn't need to worry about her body, while I let my mind drift to my brother and Stacey.

Did I want them to be together in the poly family I always thought we would have and share? I should, I knew it in my heart, but there was an unsettling, niggling sensation lurking in the back of my mind that I couldn't quite put my finger on.

David and I'd grown up knowing we'd probably share the same wife, but we'd never tried it until now. Always dateing separate women, we'd never even tried to love the same one.

Can we share a woman like Tanner and Wade do? Will we have issues like Markus and Oliver did in the beginning? Surely, there has to be teething issues with this sort of arrangement?

I stayed another hour or so, hoping to catch another glimpse of Stacey, but in the end, I headed home to an empty house. David wasn't there and neither was his car. When I tried his cell phone, it went straight to voicemail and the Bailey's was closed, and I wasn't going to disturb my parents this late. So, with nothing else to do, I heated up some leftovers and turned in earlier than usual, wanting the time to pass quickly so I could see my mate again.

Instead, I ended up lying on my back in bed unable to sleep, just listening to the soft sounds of cars and people around our neighborhood. We were close to town, too close in some ways. The house had worked for the past ten years while we were single and wanting to get to the restaurant and medical clinic running quickly, but now... maybe a larger property would be better for my child?

My child...

Those two words hadn't been ones I'd thought I'd be saying or thinking about really for a long time.

Would Stacey's baby be a girl or a boy? Would she want to breastfeed? I was a huge advocate for a woman's right to choose from a doctor's perspective, but something primal—the shifter in me—yearned to see our infant at her breast.

She'd lost a lot of weight since I'd last seen her, which meant her pregnancy hadn't been easy on her. So even if I couldn't get David to go and see her tomorrow, I'd get her into the clinic for an ultrasound, just to be safe and make sure she and the baby were okay. There wouldn't be anyone there on a Sunday, but I had keys to everything, and I'd let the clinic manager know in case she came running in. Agatha was a great manager, but she ran a tight ship.

I stayed awake well into the early hours thinking about where we'd live after the baby was born. I resolved to go straight to the real estate agents in the morning to get a jump-start on our future.

When I finally fell asleep, I sent up a little heartfelt prayer of gratitude. I was going to be a father, and it was all thanks to Stacey. She had conceived my child and kept it safe even when she didn't know where I was.

She could have lost the baby or chosen to terminate...

And I never would have known, but against all odds, she'd found me, and I would forever repay that strength and courage with kindness, and the love I knew was destined to grow and blossom between us. And I just had to trust that our perfect pairs bond would make itself known when the time was right.

I'd been around long enough to know that the path to lasting love was not always a straight one. Sometimes it was fraught with curves, kinks, and broken pavers along the way. And regardless of what we might face moving forward, we'd do it together.

CHAPTER 6
DAVID

After my chaotic run through the woods, I shared a quiet dinner with my parents and then stayed in my old room for the night. Mom and Dad didn't ask why I wasn't driving the three minutes back home. Instead, Dad had just poured me a double shot of whiskey, Mom put fresh sheets on my old bed, and I'd gone to bed early.

My heart hurt, like my chest was somehow too small for it. Tommy was going to be a father, and I was going to be a... what? An uncle? "Oh, my fucking... God!" I ran my fingers through my hair even as I lay in the old double bed, the lumpy mattress a testament to the decades that had passed since anyone had slept in this room.

I was never meant to be an uncle to *anyone's* kids except my sister, who had unfortunately never found the right man, so she was the one looking forward to being an auntie. And Tommy and I had planned to give my parents the grandchildren they had always craved, and my sister the kids she so desperately wanted to dote on in her life. But now my brother had found a woman and started a family without me.

"This wasn't the plan, Tommy. Fuck," I moaned into the darkness. My whole life, I'd looked forward to *our* life. Our shared life. Our perfect pairs life. Our family. Our mate. Our kids.

What the hell am I going to do now?

~

THE NEXT MORNING, I slept until noon, having not fallen asleep until God knows what time in the early hours of the morning.. I'd been restless as hell and eventually had passed out from sheer frustration into a dreamless black sleep.

Mom poured me a cup of coffee and pushed a plate of golden scrambled eggs and crisp toast across the counter.

I picked up a fork and took a bite, groaning at the buttery, seasoned perfection. "How are your eggs still better than mine?" I asked with a sigh. I was the one who owned a restaurant, but it seemed I couldn't touch a mother's love.

She merely winked at me and went back to getting the bacon ready for my dad.

"Morning," Dad said as he walked into the kitchen and slapped me on the back. "Restaurant closed today too?"

I shook my head. "Nah. I'll be opening at five."

"Oh, good. So you'll have time."

"For what?" I asked, taking a sip of my too sweet coffee.

"For the ultrasound," he said matter-of-factly.

That too sweet coffee burst straight from my lips and all over Mom's clean countertop.

"David!" Mom admonished, coming straight over with a washrag and a disinfectant spray. "What did you do that for?"

I was breathing hard, doggedly trying to swallow down the remaining coffee in my mouth so I didn't die from lack of air. "Um..." I coughed. "You know about the—"

"The baby? Yeah," Mom said, wiping up my mess without

complaint. "What I don't know is why you're hiding in our house like a coward."

"Whoa, love. Easy," Dad said, sitting on the stool beside me, giving me a moment to recover from the gut punch Mom's forthright words had delivered. "It's only been a night."

"Yeah, Mom." I said, sounding like a petulant teenager. "Go easy. It's only been..."

Mom's eye roll was louder than the words I was going to say, so I shut my mouth.

She cleaned up without further comment, grimacing all the while.

Dad and I exchanged glances as we waited for Mom to make her point, but she was taking her time.

She fussed about, cleaning up and rinsing out the cloth.

So, with nothing else to do, I forced myself to eat some more of my breakfast, though my stomach hurt with every forkful of eggs I shoveled down my throat.

How long have they known about Tommy and his new baby? Since I arrived last night? Why didn't they say anything?

But the answers to those questions were too daunting to truly contemplate, so I just continued to maintain my silence. No one gave me the truth like my parents, my mother especially. And I wasn't sure I could cope with a dose of her reality at the moment, though I wasn't going to run from it, either.

Mom finally turned around and leaned on the counter with both hands pressing into the wooden top. "Sweetheart, do you know for certain that Stacey isn't your mate?"

I opened my mouth to say, *"No. Of course not..."* But the warning glint in my mother's blue eyes stopped me.

"You don't know yet, David. So, don't throw away this chance at happiness... of love... for the sake of your wounded pride." She reached out and cupped my cheek, then gave me a little slap. "Now, enough moping. Go to that ultrasound."

I looked down at my plate. "That baby isn't mine, Mom."

She tapped my chin to make me lift my head. "And?"

"And? She isn't my mate," I said, feeling my anger twist and twirl in my gut. "She probably isn't even Tommy's, or he would have known the moment he met her."

Mom's lips twisted, and I saw her squash a thought, which was most unlike her.

"What?" I asked, my brow furrowing.

She shrugged nonchalantly. "You don't know everything, kiddo. Only Fate knows what's in store for you."

I glanced between my mom and dad,

He was up and pouring himself a glass of water by the sink.

"What do you two know that I don't?"

"Nothing," she answered. "But we're not going to sit by and let you throw your life away."

I groaned. "This isn't *my* life, Mom. It's Tommy's. Stacey is *his* lover. Her baby is his baby!"

"And what about Nancy's babies? Hmm?" Mom fired back. "Whose perfect pair babies are hers? Are they Wade's or Tanners? Does it matter?"

I opened my mouth to answer and realized I didn't in fact know and neither did they. And they probably didn't care one damn bit.

Mom tapped her watch emphatically. "Tick tock, son. You're going to miss it."

I began to think of every conceivable reason I shouldn't go. "But..."

"Go," Mom said firmly, putting on her authoritative parent voice. And there was no arguing with that one.

"Fine."

Fuck!

I grabbed my keys and headed out the door.

Bloody parents.

They couldn't possibly know what the right thing was for me. And they were totally wrong. It *did* matter that the baby wasn't mine. I wasn't even there for the conception, which at least Tanner and Wade had shared, I assumed.

Despite the fact that I'd always thought I'd live with Tommy in a family, we'd never had a single threesome. It seemed stupid in hindsight, but we just assumed we'd be like most perfect pair twins, and we'd find our mate and get married. Full stop. End of story. Once again, stupid. There *had* to be more to it than that.

How could we have been so naïve?

I jumped in my car and headed home. There was no way I was going to the medical clinic. I'd grab some clothes and go stay at the motel. It wasn't like I couldn't afford it. But I had a shift starting in four hours, and I needed a shower and my work clothes. But my car didn't park itself outside my house. Instead, I somehow ended up outside the clinic and the lights were on inside.

"Shit!" I hit the steering wheel with my palms and groaned. "No! Fate be damned, I'm not getting out." I cringed just hearing myself. I sounded like a petulant teen. But I couldn't sit here without getting out of my car. Even I wasn't that stubborn or stupid.

I slid out and marched up to the door. It would likely be locked, and I didn't have my cell phone on me, so I wouldn't be able to call my brother to let him know I was here. So, then I'd go home. But my heart pounded against my chest, refusing to be quiet, and I couldn't calm the fear that threatened to consume me.

What was the worst thing that could possibly happen here? I'd find out she wasn't my mate after all, and she was here just for Tommy? Or that she'd refuse to even consider me?

I didn't know, but I wasn't a coward, and I'd prove it. I lifted my hand and knocked on the door stubbornly. I waited for two whole seconds then turned to leave.

There, I did it.

The door opened, and my brother was standing on the other side with his eyes wide and his jaw practically hanging open. "You're here."

"Mom and Dad thought I should come and see how my..." I gulped at the lump that lodged firmly in my throat. "Neice or nephew is doing." The sadness I saw sweep over Tommy's face was heavy enough that it made me look away. I couldn't bear that kind of disappointment on top of what I was already feeling.

"Well, come in. We're just getting set up." Tommy waved me in.

I took a deep breath, then walked inside the clinic and glanced around the waiting room. "You painted," I said, gesturing at the new light blue walls. The waiting room had been a crisp, sterile white for years. This felt much more welcoming and relaxing by comparison. It somehow settled the nerves.

"Yeah, we did," he answered simply. "Come on, brother." Tommy patted me on the shoulder encouragingly.

I walked down the hallway to the room at the end and followed him in.

Inside, Stacey was waiting, sitting on top of the table.

As soon as I entered the room, I lost my breath. She was so beautiful that my shifter howled inside my mind like a lunatic.

"Hi, David," she said, smiling hesitantly at me.

"Hello," I replied, shoving my wolf down as I stepped around one side of the table, away from all the machines. Her belly was huge, a lot bigger than I'd realized previously. "I'm sorry I didn't stick around yesterday." I didn't touch her, though my skin tingled with anticipation.

She chuckled softly and ran her hands over her baby bump. "It's okay, and I don't blame you. Yesterday was really full on."

I just nodded because what else could I do?

Tommy turned on the monitor and grabbed a paddle. "Just lie back and get comfortable, Stacey. Lift your top."

She grimaced a little as she leaned back, shifting as though uncomfortable, then raised her tight black t-shirt. Her belly was round and odd... and strangely perfect.

"All right, let's see how everything is going," Tommy said as he applied clear gel and ran the probe over Stacey's belly.

They both turned to look at the screen to discern the grainy image that appeared.

I couldn't help but stare at Stacey's hair, mesmerized by its glistening gold tones even beneath the stark indoor lighting.

"Okay, we're measuring at twenty-six weeks, which puts the dates right in line with the conference," Tommy confirmed, smiling at Stacey with relief.

They shared a moment and a flush of crimson rose in Stacey's cheeks as she obviously remembered their night together.

Cold terror hit me in my belly unexpectedly, and I realized my mistake. This was too personal. I was intruding on their private moment, and I needed to leave as soon as possible. An uncle's place wasn't at his brother's lover's bedside.

I shouldn't have come.

I stumbled forward awkwardly, eager to escape such a confronting situation. "Ah... I should go. This is for you two, not for me. It was nice to meet you again, Stacey." I waved toward her, hoping against hope that I had my poker face in place. I couldn't have her see just how crushed I was. None of this was her fault.

Catching me unaware, she reached out, grabbing my arm as I passed the bed. "No. David, stay," she said calmly.

Electricity coursed through my body, making my skin tingle and my legs shake under me.

"What was that?" Stacey asked, gently taking her hand away

and looking down at her palm with a perplexed expression, as though she might have felt something similar to what I had just experienced.

"Hey, brother, are you okay?" Tommy asked, his brow furrowed as he turned his gaze to me.

But I was unable answer. In the next heartbeat my legs buckled and gave out from underneath me, and to my everlasting shame I hit the deck like a freaking sack of potatoes. I couldn't believe it. My mind reeled with shock. The perfect pairs stories were true! And not just for others, but for me too.

Well, I'll be fucked.

CHAPTER 7
TOMMY

Watching my brother fall to his knees like he'd been struck in the heart by our beautiful woman was amazingly satisfying. We'd heard stories from the other perfect pairs our whole lives about their first meetings with their mates, but we hadn't *really* believed that it would happen for us. It seemed absurd that the mere touch of a woman could bring great wolf shifters to their knees. But here it was, happening right there in front of me. The proof was most definitely in the proverbial pudding.

"Are you okay?" Stacey asked my brother, her expression creased in concern, further revealing her sweet and empathetic nature.

David was staring mutely down at the ground as though it contained the answers to life. His chest rose and fell with each labored breath as he tried desperately to make sense of what had just taken place between him and our mate.

Come on, brother. Look up!

David groaned after a time before he managed an answer. "Ah... I think so."

I put the ultrasound wand down and walked around the hospital bed, extending a hand to David, who was still firmly on his knees. "Come on, brother. We still haven't seen our baby yet."

David lifted his head, and within his eyes I saw everything I'd ever hoped for—for him and us. He was filled with wild excitement and a blazing hope that burned like the sun, mingled with just a touch of fear. All emotions very befitting our present scenario.

David nodded once, resolute, and accepted my hand, climbing to his feet with a rough cough.

I wanted to shout with excitement and joy as the realization of our perfect pairs bond washed over me, but Stacey hadn't officially said that she'd even be with me again, let alone accept David as her mate. Our collective focus should be on the baby, and the needs of our mate, so we needed to keep the spotlight there for now. "All right, now that David's on his feet…" I trailed off with a smile.

"Sit next to me," Stacey said, reaching out for him.

David took her hand, shivering at her touch, then collapsing on to the chair next to her with another shiver, his gaze a little glassy.

I smothered the amiable laugh that rose in my throat, but I couldn't stop the smile that filled my heart at seeing my brother so clearly stupefied and besotted with Stacey.

Stacey was staring at me warmly, waiting for me to continue.

So, I put the wand back on her belly and began the measurements once more. "The baby is looking very healthy, Stacey." I said, measuring the length of the femur and looking for any signs of concern.

"There's only one?" she asked.

I chuckled. "Oh, yes. One healthy…"
Girl.

My stomach tightened with excitement. A little girl to adore and spoil! "Do you want to know the gender?" I asked her, finding it hard to contain my excitement.

"Do you know what it is?" she replied, her eyebrows rising.

I nodded. "Yes, I'm sorry. At twenty-six weeks, it's impossible for me not to see."

"Well, if you know, I want to know," she said, anticipating the answer.

I glanced over to my brother, noting his curiosity piqued. Then I looked back to Stacey. "You're going to have a little girl."

"Oh my God! How lovely!" Stacey gushed, smiling down at her big belly, a beautiful and pure light in her eyes. "I wasn't sure, of course, but I had a feeling."

"Why..." David's voice broke, so he cleared it loudly before continuing. "Why haven't you been able to get medical care before now, Stacey?"

She sighed. "Well, I was working as a contractor, so got no benefits. Then I was moving around and lost my job due to the pregnancy, and I've just been... surviving, really. I never stopped looking for Tommy and trying to get enough money together to get here."

David stood up, staring at the screen, a look of hardened resolve on his face. "How long do we have to prepare, Tommy? Three months?"

I nodded in confirmation. "Yeah, give or take."

David nodded and walked over to the door. "I have to go get ready for work, but will you both come in for dinner? I'd like to show Stacey the restaurant." David smiled at Stacey, but I could feel his nerves and anxiety as if they were my own.

"Your restaurant?" she queried, wiping the gel from her belly with the towel I'd handed her.

He nodded. "Yes, Tommy will explain. I've got to run. But I'll see you tonight?"

"You will," she answered.

And then David was gone.

Stacey tugged her top back down over her blossoming bump and offered me a lop-sided smile. "He's a bit intense."

I laughed. "He's my brother, so you're not going to get an unbiased answer or argument from me there."

She grinned and swung her legs off the table. "Yeah, I didn't have siblings growing up, but I kind of get that 'We don't get along, but touch them and die' type of loyalty vibe here." She sounded almost sad about it.

I couldn't help but wonder why and what her experiences growing up had been like, but now didn't seem like the appropriate time to address that. Instead, I laughed. "You got that right. My brother and I often butt heads, but we're a team through and through. It's us against the world, and if anyone tried to hurt our older sister..." I whistled and shook my head with amusement at the thought. "Touch her and die would definitely apply!"

Stacey's head swung up and stared at me, her eyes wide. "You have a sister?"

"Yeah. Her name's Allie. She's a few years older than us."

Stacey hopped to her feet and smoothed down her top properly. "Is she married with kids?" she asked.

I shook my head and turned off the ultrasound machine. "No. Unfortunately, she never met the right guy. But she *always* wanted kids, so once she finds out about you? You'll be smothered with love and kindness and have gained a new best friend. She'll be the most doting auntie you could ever imagine. Just warning you!"

Tears swam in Stacey's eyes as she gulped back unspoken emotions and nodded. "That would be... really nice."

I reached out and pulled her into my arms, holding her close and enjoying the tiny sparks of recognition within my skin. This woman was definitely our mate, and although I was *so* happy and relieved to have found her, I couldn't believe I hadn't recognized her in the beginning.

I really was stinking drunk. Jesus.

"Do you want go back to our house and see our place?" I asked her, rubbing her back protectively. "You can take a rest if you want, then we can go out to the steakhouse for dinner?"

Stacey pulled back and looked up at me, wiping the tears from her cheeks. "Bailey's Steakhouse? Is that the restaurant David owns?"

I nodded. "Yes, and I'm sure the iron would do you good. Pregnancy takes a lot of energy, and I'm sure your little girl would love a steak."

We started walking towards the door when she corrected me. "Our little girl, you mean, right? You're not going to turn us away, are you?"

I stopped walking and gently turned her toward me, gripping her arms as softly as I could with such urgency pulsing through my veins. "Stacey, I'm never letting either of you go, ever again. If I'd known how important you were in the beginning, I probably wouldn't have slept long enough for you to get away."

Her brow furrowed. "What do you mean about me being important? Do you mean... because I'm carrying the baby?"

I shook my head, a sliver of fear slicing through me.

Shit. She hasn't entirely put the pieces of the puzzle together yet.

"No... I mean, you and I are *meant* to be together. My family, as you know, the perfect pairs... we share our mates... our wives. And you already know that we have insane amounts of chemistry."

She gulped, trembling ever so slightly under my touch. "Yeah, but you mean—"

"That reaction David had? Where he hit the deck after you touched him?"

She nodded, her lip quivering as she absorbed my words and drew her own conclusions.

I pushed on. Even though I knew it was too early in our relationship to tell her everything, it was too late in her pregnancy—in our life—to hold anything back now. We were committed, and this was happening. "Well, that means that you're *our* mate. Our Fated soulmate, David's and mine, if you believe in such things."

She wrapped her arms around herself, looking defensive. "Well, I do in theory, but you can't really feel something like that, can you?"

"We can," I said, wanting to reveal to her that we were wolf shifters, but at the same time worried it would be too much all at once. "So, I want you. Forever. You and our baby will be my whole world now."

"And David?" she whispered, her eyes growing big and wide, glistening like a doe's.

"He wants you too," I said with a grin. "He just won't admit it yet. He's a touch stubborn like that."

"Even with the... you know, the *zappy* thing?" she asked.

I laughed at her description. It was definitely a *zing* or a *zap*. "The reason for the *zappy* thing is so that we don't miss our soulmate when we meet them. I unfortunately didn't feel it as much the night we met because I'd had so much to drink, and I think it dulled my senses. But I feel it now. There's no denying it, not even if I wanted to." I reached out and cupped her face gently.

She tilted her head up in invitation, her expression surprisingly serene and trusting.

Without reservation, I leaned forward, gently kissing her perfect lips. I didn't linger long, not wanting to make this moment about sex or passion. The love and connection I wanted us to share with would run deep and last forever. There would be plenty of time for physical fun later. Right now, I just wanted to make sure she felt safe and wanted. Truly wanted. I broke our chaste kiss with a tender smile.

"I—" Stacey said, then cleared her throat. "I don't know what to say."

"You don't have to say anything," I said gently. "We've got all the time in the world. And now that you've found me, we can build a life together, assuming that's what you want?" I allowed the words to sound like a question, but my heart would shrivel up and die if she said that it wasn't what she wanted. That she came here for financial support for the baby and nothing more.

She nodded slowly and chewed her lower lip. "I'd like that. It would be what's best for the baby, I think."

I put my hand against the small of her back. "It will be best for *all* of us, Stacey. I know it. But there's no hurry to make anything official if it makes you feel uncomfortable. We can just get to know each other and let things grow organically. No stress. We'll just take it all as it comes... together." I opened the front door to the clinic and guided her out into the fresh morning air.

"That would be lovely," she said, but once we got to the car, she turned to me with a grimace. "Do you mind if I go back to Nancy's house for a few hours? I'm feeling a little dizzy. Maybe I could see your house some other time?"

"Of course," I said, helping her into the car before getting in myself. "Are you still okay to go out for dinner? I'll explain to David that you can't if you're not feeling up to it."

My brother would be disappointed if that were the case, but this wasn't about him, and I knew instinctively that he'd accept it without question, especially now that our bond had been revealed. This was about the woman we were both meant to love, and the daughter that was soon coming into our life.

"Ah... the steakhouse would be nice," she said, not reneging on her promise to David that she'd be there. "If you give me your cell number, I can let you know when I'm awake again."

"Perfect," I said.

I drove her back home to Nancy's and walked her to the door, but she didn't ask me to come inside. In fact, she seemed like she wanted me to go, so I did. But not before I had her cell number and she had mine. I'd almost lost the chance to be with my mate due to bad timing and a serious case of inebriation, and I wasn't going to lose her again.

Fate was giving me a second chance not to cock this up, and I wouldn't fail her this time. I would be the partner, lover, friend, and father she needed me to be. I'd support her no matter what. And together, between my brother and I, she wouldn't want for anything. She'd have love, security, and a large and fiercely loyal family to back her through hell or high water. And our baby— our daughter—would be the most adored little girl in the world.

CHAPTER 8

STACEY

I closed the door on Tommy, my heart full to aching with happiness and turmoil. My baby was a little girl, and she was healthy and well. The news couldn't have been better. A healthy baby was all any mother wanted after all, and yet there was so much that remained unknown. I wasn't quite sure how to process it all. My life had turned upside down over the course of a mere twenty-four hours, which was wonderful and frightening all at once.

"How'd it go?" Nancy asked, walking up to me holding her mug of peppermint tea. She didn't go far without the one thing that helped her nausea, and I understood that all too well.

"Good, I think," I said, chewing on my lip as I debated whether to share our news before deciding I should. "We're going to be having a little girl."

"Oh, congratulations!" Nancy cried, throwing an arm around me, and hugging me gently but enthusiastically. "I'm so happy for you, Stacey. That's wonderful."

I rubbed my hands over my bump, enjoying the way the baby

was kicking—lively, strong, and healthy. She was obviously excited.

"You want a cup of tea?" Nancy asked, gesturing toward the kitchen.

I nodded and followed her, loving the feel of her peaceful and happy space.

"The boys went out," Nancy explained. "So, for now, it's just us." She moved to the cupboard, pulled down a mug and some more tea bags, then started making me a soothing beverage.

I sat on a stool and waited patiently, just basking in the tranquility of the moment despite some of my niggling worries.

When Nancy finally turned back around, she handed me a cup, pulled out a packet of cookies and smiled. "All right, spill! What's going on in your head? I can tell something's up."

I wrapped my hands around the mug, reveling in the welcome heat against my skin. "I don't think I quite get this whole perfect pairs *thing*."

Nancy grinned at me as if that was precisely what she had been expecting me to say. "Yeah, it's pretty weird in the beginning, isn't it?"

I nodded my head and took a sip of the tea to try and calm my doubts, but when I put the mug back down, the anxiety in my head and my heart was still there.

"I was freaked out by it in the beginning too, trust me," Nancy admitted. "I mean, two men and me? Oh my God. At the time I couldn't even fathom it. But life with them is *amazing*. They're the best team, and the most incredible husbands anyone could ever wish for. I have never been happier. No matter what, I know that they're both here for me and that's beyond comforting. You can't buy that kind of peace."

I sighed. "The thing is, I don't know if David wants me, or even if I want to become part of this poly... three... deal."

Nancy laughed but it was a happy sound, not a derogatory

one. "You sound like you just need some more information, hon. What have they told you so far? Maybe I can help clear things up for you. I do have firsthand experience in this department, after all."

I took a sip of my tea and sighed, willing to let her at least try and help out. "Well, David's barely spoken to me, but Tommy seems to think I'm his mate... or something."

Mate. What a weird word to use.

Soulmate seemed okay, I supposed. You heard that term bandied about in romantic contexts, in books, movies, and greeting cards. But there was something *else*, like a hidden meaning behind his words, I could tell.

"And David's mate too?' Nancy asked, her smile growing larger by the second.

I shrugged. "Well, Tommy thinks so. When I put my hand on David's, he kind of fell down." Which had been the strangest thing to witness, but also sort of funny. It had reminded me of those childhood cartoons where someone got hit on the head with a frying pan, making their head spin and their eyes go all googly.

Nancy clapped and practically did a little jump of joy, almost spilling her tea. "Oh my God, Stacey! That's *so* great! Okay. So, you're both of their mates, and we just have to work out the whole baby being Tommy's and not David's thing."

I stared at her.

Sorry... what? Hold up!

"Um, I don't even know if I want David for sure. We haven't even had the chance to get to speak to each other properly, so why does everyone assume that I'll jump into this weird—no offense—poly relationship?"

Nancy waved her hand, not in the least perturbed. "No offense taken. And the honest answer is because you won't find more amazing men on the planet. A perfect pair's devotion to their mate is the stuff dreams are literally made of. You won't find men who will love you more or love your baby more. I don't want to push you one way or another, but there's no way you'll be able to refuse them once they start seducing you."

I rolled my eyes at her. "Well, *obviously*, I already succumbed. Just look at me."

Tommy had seduced me with a single damn look. A single word! He was still the most handsome man I'd ever seen, though David wasn't far behind. Each of them had their own unique appeal, so it was tough to compare them that way, really. They were sort of, well, complimentary when I thought about it.

Nancy put her hand out and tapped the marble counted with her fingernails. "I know you're worried and a bit freaked out, but please, give them the chance. If you ever dreamed of a happily ever after with a husband, a house, babies... this is it. If you've got the courage to take it—and I think you do."

I gulped down the emotions that rose within me. "What makes you say that? How can you be so sure?"

"Because you're here!" she exclaimed, throwing her arms out wide. "You found Tommy against all odds, pregnant and alone. And I know you've got more of a story than you're admitting to, but you can share it all with me whenever you're ready. But my point is, you could have made *so* many other choices, and yet with a nudge from Fate, you came here."

I rolled my eyes again and sighed as I took another sip of my tea. "Yeah. Fate. She hasn't been so kind to me in the past."

My first husband... my old family, finances... and my career.

"Well, if you stick around, I'm pretty sure you're going to see that you're in the right place." Nancy's smile was cheeky, satisfied, and smug as she grabbed a cookie to chomp down on.

Nancy had said "if," but I knew full well I wasn't going anywhere. Even if Tommy came to his senses and realized that I wasn't good enough for him, I would be staying in town. My baby—my daughter—deserved a family, and I knew I couldn't give her everything she deserved on my own. I believed in the age-old adage "it takes a village". Life was always better when you had a community of those you could trust behind you.

"I hope you don't mind, but I think I'm going to go lie down for a while," I said, pushing off the chair and wincing at the pain that shot through my butt. My back was ridiculously sore. I really needed to rest and stretch out.

"Go for it," Nancy said, waving at me as I waddled away. "Are you here for dinner?" she called after me.

"Ah, no," I said, holding my belly as it grew heavier with each step, "Tommy's taking me to David's restaurant."

Nancy grinned at me. "It's really nice there. You'll enjoy it!"

I took my world-weary body and trundled up the stairs, taking her word for it. I was asleep before my head hit the pillow and didn't wake up until the sun had gone down.

My aching back woke me up, and although I was tempted to just roll over, resettle and go back to sleep, a niggling need to get up and check my phone stole over me. I managed to get up out of bed and saw that it was past six o'clock in the evening. "Shit."

Tommy had already messaged me twice, but he hadn't called, probably not wanting to wake me in case I was still sleeping.

I quickly messaged him back to say that I'd just woken up and if he could give me half an hour to shower and change, I'd be ready for dinner.

He messaged straight back to say he hadn't called because he was afraid to wake me and that he'd see me in thirty minutes.

I chuckled as I waddled to the bathroom in all my six-month-pregnant glory. I didn't doubt that when he said thirty minutes, he meant to the second, so I couldn't dawdle. I undressed as fast as my burgeoning form would allow and stepped into the shower.

It hadn't escaped my attention that I didn't deserve a man like Tommy. An accomplished, gorgeous man.

A freaking doctor of all things! What girl doesn't dream of landing a doctor?

And there was a huge part of me that hated the fact that I'd fallen pregnant and now he had to deal with me forever. I felt guilty as hell if I was being honest. I'd just lobbed into his life, and he was expected by one and all to be a gentleman and take me in like a stray kitten. I sighed as the hot water ran over my aching muscles.

The horrible feelings of doubt and insecurity kept coming as I washed my expanding body and got dressed into one of the three outfits I owned that still fit me. A simple black maternity dress I'd found at a thrift shop. It was definitely the nicest thing I had. Running a comb through my long locks, and adding a quick lick of lip gloss, I'd just managed to get my sandals on and walk downstairs to find Wade chatting with Tommy in the living room.

"Hey," I said, smiling at the man who was practically beaming at me.

"Tommy says you guys are having a girl. Congrats!" Wade said.

"Thanks," I answered, holding my belly protectively as I so often did. "It's nice to know, actually. I wasn't sure I wanted to initially, but now..." I shrugged. "I'm happy."

Little girls' names had occupied my thoughts since early on in the pregnancy, pretty, traditional ones like Maragaret and Daphne. But for months now I'd been forced to focus on surviving, and I hadn't really cared what gender the baby turned out to be. It had only mattered ultimately that they were healthy when they arrived.

"Are you ready to go?" Tommy asked. "You look great."

"Thanks," I said. "You do, too." My gaze roamed over the beauty that was the father of my child. He was wearing a casual white linen shirt and a pair of perfectly fitted blue jeans that made me want to take a photo and put it on a bulletin board for everyone to admire. He was literally front cover magazine material.

"Let's go then," he said, opening the front door and holding out his hand for me to take.

I waved goodbye to Wade and took hold of Tommy's hand. "Thanks for picking me up."

"Of course," he said, not letting go of my hand as we walked down the sidewalk to the curb.

I stared at the huge black SUV, much like the one Nancy had. "Is this your car?" I asked.

"It is now," he replied with a grin, opening the passenger side door as he did so. "After I dropped you off, I went car shopping this afternoon. I figured we needed something a little more family friendly." His smile was so genuine and beautiful it brought tears to my eyes. He was already changing and adapting to being a father without complaint or having been asked.

He is so amazing.

I gulped back the emotions that wanted to unravel me into a blithering, hormonal mess and managed an answer. "But it's Sunday. Who was open today?"

Tommy shrugged casually. "A patient of mine owns the car dealership in town. He did me a favor. Hop in."

I slid into the car, breathing in the new car scent while Tommy shut the door and hurried around to the driver's side. My eyes were hot and filling with tears, and I had to focus on calming down so I didn't ruin the evening.

"Are you all right?" Tommy asked as he turned on the ignition.

I nodded, holding back a sniffle. "Yes. I'm just impressed you went out and bought this car for us. It was thoughtful."

He laughed, and it was like music to my ears. "I've been waiting for you for decades, Stacey. And this baby is a dream come true. I can't wait to meet my little girl."

I gripped my belly, my forced laugh shuddering in my chest over the serious notes in what Tommy was saying. "Well, *I* can. I'm not looking forward to the birth."

Tommy reached out and gripped my hand. "I'll get you the best OB around, Stacey. We'll take care of you, I promise."

"Good, because I want drugs," I said, "Lots of drugs. Pain and I are not friends." I didn't have healthcare, so there was no way I could afford a luxury birth. Not in the country, especially.

"Whatever you want, you can have," Tommy assured me as if it were the most obvious thing in the world to treat the mother of his baby like a literal queen. "But first, dinner."

We drove to the Steak House, and I fidgeted the whole way. I'd hoped Tommy would want to help me with our child when I went searching for him, but he was acting like he was ready to change his whole life just to be with us. It was more than I'd ever dared hope for. It was definitely in the realm of dreams...

And if this is one, I'm not sure I ever want to wake up!

CHAPTER 9

DAVID

Work proved the perfect refuge from the crazy thoughts racing through my mind like sugar-crazed bees. It was Sunday night, so the steakhouse was at full capacity, and my staff was running around like their pants were on fire—just how I'd trained them. Fast and efficient without compromising on quality or service.

Tammy, my restaurant manager, popped her head into the kitchen and got my attention. "Chef, your brother's here," she called.

My heart pounded faster, my throat becoming tight in an instant. I nodded my head at Tammy before answering, buying a second to compose myself. "I reserved a booth in the back for them," I replied.

She smiled. "I saw Tommy's name in the schedule. I'll seat them myself."

I got back to work but began to make mistakes as my anxiety ramped up knowing my mate was nearby, right here in my establishment.

"Chef, this meal was returned," Sally, one of my waitresses

said, offering me an apologetic look. "They ordered the special without mushrooms."

I stared down at the plate and sighed. "I need a break. Sous-chef! I'm going on break."

"I'm here, Chef!" Harold stepped up next to me. "Would you like dinner brought out?"

My brother and Stacey's meals had just gone out, so I could probably go and eat with them if I wanted to. "Yes, thank you," I answered as I unwrapped my apron and went to the bathroom to wash my face and put on a new shirt. I was sweaty from slaving over the industrial stoves, and to be honest, I was getting more anxious just thinking about sitting within touching distance of Stacey.

Will that horrible zappy, tingly thing happen every time she touches me?

I seriously hoped not, and for my sanity I had to assume it wouldn't. My cousins didn't hit the deck every time their mates touched them, and Tommy didn't seem to have a problem with it at all.

I quickly redressed, slicked my hair back, and walked into the restaurant smiling and waving at the patrons who immediately lit up, seeing the owner out of the kitchen. I made a bee line for the booth I'd organized Stacey and Tommy to be seated in. The booth was dark compared to the others and the most private, which suited our unique situation best.

They were both chatting and eating, laughing as she sipped water and he on wine. Stacey's skin glowed in the low mood lighting and her hair shone like she'd been moon-kissed.

With more courage than I felt, I stepped up to the table and cleared my throat.

Stacey looked up at me and smiled as bright as the sun. She was literally radiant. The rest at Nancy's had clearly been much needed.

My wolf howled in my mind, and I lost my ability to talk. I'd always hoped that when I met my mate, I'd know. That the recognition would be instantaneous, and that we'd fall together, in love and into bed.

Stacey leaned back in the booth, pressing a hand to her belly, which was swollen with Tommy's growing child.

My ability to speak came back immediately with that cold dose of reality, and I slid into my professional role, the easiest of my personalities to choose. "Are you enjoying your meal?" I asked, offering my mate a polite smile in return.

She nodded. "Oh, yes, thank you. It's perfect. Are you going to sit with us?"

I was halfway toward changing my mind about that, but Anthony was already walking our way from the kitchen with my plate in hand.

"Ah, yes, if that's all right? I thought I'd take a short break."

"Of course! Please, sit," she said, sliding along the bench seat in a quick move I wasn't expecting, given her current condition.

"Oh..." I glanced over at my brother, who hadn't moved, whereas Stacey had made room for me beside her. "Thanks."

What else could I say? I slid into the booth alongside Tommy's pregnant mate—*our* mate—and took up the knife and fork that Anthony had placed down for me. "Thanks, Anthony."

The waiter nodded and took his leave, dutifully returning to the kitchen for the next round of orders.

I took a moment to glance around the restaurant, which was still full and thankfully running well. At least I'd make a good impression with my business.

Good.

"So, how was the rest of your day?" I asked the table, trying not to stare at Stacey even though I was aching to do so.

"I called Tony and bought a new SUV," Tommy announced.

I chewed on my steak, barely tasting it.

Tommy traded in his beloved sports car for a family van?

"Nice," I said casually when I couldn't think of anything more to offer. I turned toward Stacey with my eyebrows raised. I needed to make a real connection with her and every chance to do so precious, even if I was still uncomfortable about how this had all unfolded. "Stacey?" I prompted.

She toyed with the stem on her wine glass that was filled with sparkling water. "I had a chat with Nancy, which was good. It's nice to have someone to talk to. Then I had a nap—I needed it."

"I can imagine," I managed to say. But truthfully, I had no idea what went on during pregnancy, nor how tired she must be, but creating another human being must surely be a hell of a lot of work and a lot of strain on the body. "I'm glad you got some rest."

"What did you talk to Nancy about?" Tommy asked.

I glared at him for a moment for interrupting before turning back to Stacey. I'd tried to purposely ignore that part of her answer. A part of me didn't want to know, and she was so tantalizingly close... I could so easily just brush against her arm or her thigh.

No! Don't touch her. She's not yours.

"Oh... ah, well, the perfect pairs thing mostly," she said, her gaze moving furtively from me to Tommy. "I had some questions."

I inhaled sharply, hating the feeling of being so far out of the loop. My ears had been burning this afternoon while I'd prepared for this evening's dinner service. I should have known they'd been talking about me. "Tommy told you about how we're supposed to share a mate?" I asked.

She stared at me, our eyes meeting with an intensity that took my breath away. "Yeah, he did. But I told Nancy that I'm not sure that will work for me, or even for you guys. Neither of you know me that well, and you probably don't like this..." She gestured to her huge belly. "So, even though it was nice to talk to Nancy, she wasn't in our situation when she met her husbands, so I just..." She trailed off, having seemingly run out of words.

I had the strangest urge to reach out and run my hand comfortingly over her huge belly, but I didn't. Again, even if Fate somehow thought this could work, it wasn't my baby, nor my right to touch her uninvited. "This is new for all of us too," I managed to say, breaking the awkward silence that hung between us. "And I can imagine *this* was a surprise for you too." I nodded toward her belly.

Tommy cleared his throat loudly, obviously wanting me to reassure Stacey that her pregnancy was indeed, wanted. I ignored him. I wasn't ready to alleviate anyone's feelings about what I thought or felt. I didn't even know yet.

"It was a surprise," Stacey said quietly, then reached out and gripped my bare forearm where my shirt was rolled up. "I'm so sorry to wreck all your plans."

My eyes slid closed on a moan I couldn't hope to contain. Her touch was the balm to my soul I'd been aching for all my life.

She didn't let go upon hearing my reaction. In fact, she gripped tighter.

The touch wasn't electric like before but was still stronger than I'd been prepared for. When I opened my eyes, she was staring at me. I didn't respond except to continue staring right back at her, just drinking in her beauty and the serenity she radiated.

"It's all true, isn't it?" she whispered, her voice trembling.

I could only nod and gulp. My chest hurt, and my immediate response was to try and get away. For some strange reason, my flight instinct was being triggered.

Somehow, she seemed to read the play and moved her hand down to my thigh. "Please stay a bit longer."

I nodded, turning quietly back to my steak and cut it into small pieces with skillful precision.

She's my mate! She really is. Oh... my... God...

But what did that mean? Would I never know her love or affection while my brother married her, and they raised their baby? Or would she include me in their life? Would I be part of a true perfect pair, or would I forever be the third wheel in their relationship?

What's the plan now?

Tommy artfully changed the subject while my brain imploded, drowning in a sea of questions. "So, Stacey, have you considered any names for the baby?"

Stacey turned to look at my brother but didn't remove her warm hand from my leg. "Sort of. I thought of a few in the beginning, but I'm not really attached to any."

"What do you like?" Tommy asked.

"Well, Margaret was my favorite," she said. "It has so many variations and Maggie is such a cute baby's name."

"I like Margaret." The words were out of my mouth before I'd given them permission to leave my brain. I glanced up to find my brother smirking at me. "What?" I protested. "It's nice."

"It is," Tommy agreed before looking back at Stacey. "Perhaps Margaret Rose, or something like that?"

"Oh, I love that," Stacey gushed, finally moving her hand back to her belly and taking a sip of her water. "That's really beautiful."

I missed her touch as soon as it was gone. It felt like a part of me had gotten up and removed itself, leaving me missing a piece. "So, where are you staying?" I asked, trying to sound casual when inside my head things were still spinning in overdrive.

"Nancy said I can stay with her for as long as I like," Stacey answered. "I don't want to be a burden, but until I can get a job here—"

"You don't need a job," I said, dismissing the notion completely. "You're carrying Tommy's baby, and you need to rest leading up to the birth, and surely for a good long while afterward. You don't need to stress, we'll take care of you."

The *"we"* was unintentional, but Tommy and I had always been a team. I wasn't going to bail on him now.

"I don't want to leech off you," she said quietly. "I do have a degree in interior design, I've just never had much chance to use it."

I reached for the bottle of red wine and poured myself a glass, needing the fortification. This conversation was already racing down avenues I hadn't planned, and Tommy wasn't helping, sitting there just smiling at me.

The smug bastard.

"We both own businesses," I said. She could redesign this whole place if she wanted to. I'd never been totally happy with the color palette anyway. "I have this restaurant and Tommy has the clinic. So, if you still feel compelled to work later, and pursue design, you're welcome to do that in either of our places. Anything you want to do, you can. But for now—"

"You need to take care of yourself and our daughter," Tommy finished for me.

I nodded and took a large sip of the wine. Had I just invited Stacey to live with us and be in our lives indefinitely? I finished my steak quickly then slid to the edge of the booth and stood. I needed time and space to think. Things were moving *very* quickly, and my instincts were making decisions my brain hadn't had the opportunity to catch up with just yet.

"I need to get back to the kitchen, but I'll see you both tomorrow maybe?"

Stacey's eyes were as round as saucers. "I really am sorry, you know. I didn't mean for this to happen. It's not what I had planned." She indicated to her belly again.

My heart broke a little when I saw the tears in her eyes. I had to be honest, even if it crushed me to admit it. She didn't deserve my pain as well as her own. "I know you didn't, and I'm not upset or mad at you. Not one bit."

"Then what is it?" she asked, sliding her hand along the table as though to reach for me.

I smiled at my own ridiculousness. "I just wish I'd been a part of it. Meeting you for the first time part and romancing you. If you're meant to be *ours*... I just feel like I should have been there. That's all. And I'm..."

Jealous.

I couldn't bring myself to say it, even if it was obvious to everyone around us.

Stacey nodded slowly as if mulling the thought over and moved her hand back to her belly.

I inclined my head in a small bow. "Enjoy the rest of your night and I'll see you both tomorrow."

I turned on my heel and returned to my kitchen, where I strived for nothing short of perfection and regularly hit the mark... unlike *everything* in my personal life, apparently.

CHAPTER 10

STACEY

Dinner was beautiful, as was David's restaurant. It was extremely sophisticated and high class for such a small town. His declaration that he was upset about having missed out on the early stages of meeting me was heart-breaking. David, despite being a perfectionist and possessing an emotionally intense personality, obviously had the biggest heart.

"What are we going to do about David?" I asked Tommy as we got out of his new car and started the short walk up to the front door of Nancy's house. I'd declined Tommy's invitation to stay at the brothers' home even though he'd told me there was an empty third bedroom that I could stay in. I just wasn't sure how I'd sleep knowing the only man to ever give me an orgasm was only one room away.

Even with my huge pregnant belly, my body wasn't exactly dormant. I still had yearnings and being around Tommy and David tonight had made me wriggle in my seat more than a few times. It would be embarrassing if I were to make a move not knowing how they felt about me.

Are they simply willing to commit and look after me because of the

baby and this pre-destined perfect pairs thing, or are they truly inter-
ested in me as a lover? Is what I'm feeling even real?

"What do you want to do about him?" Tommy asked in return with a grin.

I put my hands on my hot cheeks. "Oh my God. This is *such* a weird conversation to be having with you. Aren't you jealous that I'm asking about your brother?"

Tommy chuckled and shook his head. "Not at all, Stacey. I grew up knowing my wife would be loved by the both of us. It's a natural and normal circumstance to me."

I gulped at the use of all those very serious words, then my own jealousy kicked in. "Oh, so you've shared girlfriends before?" I ventured.

He shook his head again as we slowed to stand on the patio outside Nancy's house. "Not at all. Never. We were waiting for you." He reached out and took my hand, drawing me closer.

I went willingly into his arms without fear or shame because it was Tommy. The only place, the only man whose arms I'd ever felt truly safe in.

He slid one hand around what was left of my waist and the other cupped my face.

I reached for him, laying my hands on his broad chest, feeling the steady beat of his heart beneath my palms.

"You are so beautiful," he whispered. Dropping his head, he pressed his lips against mine, kissing me softly.

My fingers curled into his shirt as I pressed myself closer, desiring a deeper kiss—more connection. Something real.

Tommy complied, reading my body language perfectly. His tongue swept between my lips, tasting me, and causing me to shiver with anticipation and wanting.

I slid my tongue against his, moaning in pleasure. Heat curled in my belly as I moved my hands up to his face, cupping his jaw before sliding them into his hair. My nipples ached, and I wished he'd touch me there.

But instead of tugging me into his body and stripping me like I wanted, he pulled back with a gentle smile, his eyes glassy with the same attraction I felt. "Damn, I wish you'd come home with me," he lamented, though there was no pressure in his words. He was simply sharing his feelings.

I swallowed hard. I wanted him too, but we'd already made it as far as Nancy's porch, and if we were going to follow our attraction to the end that it so desperately desired, I wanted to be better prepared. "Maybe tomorrow?" I answered with a rueful smile.

He nodded. "There's no rush. I don't want you to feel stressed or pushed into anything. Besides, hopefully we've got the rest of our lives, right?"

I laughed. "Right... yeah, I guess," I said, not willing promise or agree to anything just yet. There were still so many uncertainties, and they niggled at me like an itch I couldn't scratch.

He kissed me again, more lightly this time. "Well, if you happen to change your mind, just text me. I can be here in three minutes." He winked and turned on his heel. "Goodnight, Stacey," he called over his shoulder.

My body slammed for me for a traitor as I waved goodbye. I needed him *so* much it was maddening. And even though my body had changed dramatically since I was last naked with Tommy, surely he wouldn't mind too much? After all, it was his baby inside me.

David...

Somehow, it didn't feel right without him. That was part of what was bothering me, I realized. I couldn't be intimate with Tommy knowing David was out in the cold, just waiting to be included. To be brought into the triangle he'd dreamed of his whole life. I sighed and as I turned around, the door flew open.

Nancy grinned at me. "I'll get a key cut for you tomorrow. I don't want you finding yourself locked out." She waved me inside.

"Thanks," I said. "But I don't want to put you out. I might not be staying too much longer anyway."

Stacey grinned. "Yeah, I figured the boys would want you close by. Do you need help packing, or..."

"I'm not moving in with them yet," I said, rolling my eyes. "I'm not *that* easy. I'm still trying to figure this out."

Stacey burst out laughing at that one. "It wouldn't matter if you were a thirty-year-old virgin. If a set of perfect pairs want you, you don't stand a chance."

I shook my head at her certainty as she led me to the kitchen to make a cup of tea.

Tanner walked into the room with a grin. "I just got a call from Markus. Lexie's in labor!"

"Oh, she'll be *so* relieved," Nancy said with a sigh. "She's been wanting that baby out of her for weeks now."

"Who's Lexie?" I asked before I gratefully accepted the cup of tea from Nancy and sat on a stool at the counter. "Thanks."

"Oh, you have to meet her!" Nancy gushed. "You'll love her. She's tough as nails, but super sweet too."

I smiled and took a sip of tea, waiting for an answer to the question I'd asked.

Tanner answered me. "Lexie is mated to our cousins, another set of perfect pairs actually."

"Three sets in one family?" I gaped at Tanner. "How many more are there?"

"That's it, here anyway," Tanner said with a grin. "Though we've got distant cousins in the Rockies, and there's three sets there too."

"Wow. That's incredible," I breathed.

And how lucky are all those women? It's like threesome city!

There was a knock at the door, and my stomach fluttered with butterflies. Was that for me? I didn't want to ask because how self-centered would that seem?

Tanner went off to answer the door, because after all, it was his house. He came back however, staring at me with a sparkle in his eye. "You've got a visitor."

I got to my feet, assuming it was Tommy coming back for another kiss or something more. But it was my handsome chef, dressed in a casual shirt and trousers. "Hey," I managed.

"Hey, David!" Nancy called out. "You want a drink? Coffee? Tea? Wine?"

He glanced over at Nancy and offered her a perfunctory smile. "Thanks, but I can't stay long. I have to get back to close up soon." Then his dark eyes slid over to me. "Can I get a moment with you, Stacey?" He seemed anxious but also very determined.

I had a feeling that was how he would often be unless our connection grew. I smiled at Nancy and took my cup of tea with me as I walked toward David, "Yeah, sure. Ah... I was about to go upstairs to lie down. Do you want to come up with me so I can take my shoes off? My feet are kind of killing me."

He nodded and his gaze flared with heat.

I swallowed the squeal that rose in my throat and made my way up the stairs and into my room without glancing backward. "The bedrooms here are huge," I said, jabbering away with nerves. "There's a full sitting room as well." I pushed open the door and indicated to the two lounge chairs. "Please, have a seat."

I set my cup of tea on the bedside table and sat on the mattress so I could pull off my sandals. As soon as I was done and my feet sank into the soft, plush carpet, I sighed. "Oh, that's better." Despite my pregnancy fatigue, I managed to get back to my feet and walk back over to where David still stood, paused in the middle of the room. "Are you okay?" I asked hesitantly.

He moved so fast I didn't see him coming. In the next instant his hands were on my face, cupping my jaw and holding me close. His mouth was a hairsbreadth from my lips and his eyes were staring straight into mine. "I need to kiss you," he said. He wasn't asking permission, that was obvious, but he was waiting. He wouldn't claim me against my will.

I melted and couldn't prevent myself from saying the only thing that made sense. "Okay."

The next moment, his lips were on mine, and I was robbed of breath, reason and sanity.

Oh, God! He tastes divine.

My eyes slid closed, and I moaned as pleasure swept through me.

David's hands moved to my arms, then down to my waist where he grabbed me and held me tight to his hard body.

I wrapped my arms around his neck, running my fingers through his long, silky hair.

He broke our kiss abruptly, making me stumble forward and onto him. His breathing was labored, his chest rising and falling. "I have to go."

"Why?" I asked, my fingers still digging into his shirt for balance, for some kind of anchor in the storm of passion I'd just found myself.

His eyebrows lowered as he stared at me. "I came here to see if you wanted me like you want Tommy."

There was only one way I was going to be able to prove to David just how much I actually wanted the man in front of me—a man I'd only met today—who lit my body on *fire*. "I want you," I said, biting into my lower lip. "But I'm afraid my belly's going to put you off."

"Show me," he said.

Fear gripped me.

Holy shit, this is really happening.

But I couldn't back out now. I'd thrown down the gauntlet, and I couldn't pick it up again. I took a step back and grabbed my dress, pulling it up and over my head before dropping the fabric on the carpet beside me. I stood before his hungry gaze in only a tiny pair of maternity panties and a bra that barely contained my overflowing breasts.

His gaze grew dark as he stepped toward me, unspeaking. His hands went to my belly, cupping both sides of the bump and staring for a moment as if concentrating before lifting his gaze to mine. "You're exquisite." Then he kissed me again, and I melted into his arms.

I wanted him *so* much, but how could I be with David while Tommy was at home? I turned one brother down tonight only to become entangled with the other.

Are there rules about this?

David's hand slid down between my thighs and my knees buckled as his fingers slid over the crotch of my panties. He caught me, his erection pressing against me. "Damn, I need you," he said, then tugged me toward the bed. He threw back the covers and knelt down so he could peel my flimsy underwear down my pale legs.

I stepped out of them, then undid my bra, letting it whisper off me and to the floor with a great sigh of relief.

David rose to his feet again. "Lie down," he whispered.

I did what he wanted, all the while wishing he'd get naked too. I yearned to see him in all his hard, muscular glory.

He kicked off his shoes and peeled the shirt from his body.

The breath caught in my throat as I stared in awe and desire at the skin he'd revealed. "You're so beautiful," I gasped.

He smiled as he climbed onto the bed beside me, his pants

still on. "Not like you," he all but purred, his voice husky with desire as he set his lips to my sensitive breast.

Can I handle two beautiful, strong, and fiercely protective men?

But the instant he sucked one rosy, pink nipple into his mouth, any remaining worries about perfect pairs or threesomes flew from my mind.

Then his hand slid back between my thighs, and I was lost. Nancy was right. Between Tommy and David, I was a goner, and their touch felt nothing but right.

CHAPTER 11
DAVID

My wolf howled inside my mind as my senses were overwhelmed by my mate's scent. Her breasts were huge and so luscious, the mere sight of them made my mouth water. I set my lips on one of her nipples and suckled her, loving the taste of her skin and the little moans and mewling sounds Stacey made as I teased her flesh.

My fingers pressed her thighs open where I found her slick, wet and ready for me. I lifted my head from her breasts and watched with rapture as she threw her head back into the pillows.

Her eyes flew open, and she grabbed the sides of my head, her gaze intense and full of lust. "Please kiss me, David," she breathed.

I slid up and kissed her hard, more than willing to give her everything she desired. Her lips were soft, but her passion was not. She was like fire, raging and burning with need and hunger.

Then her hands were on my body, gripping my biceps and pressing into my chest. She gasped and groaned, her brazen and unashamed yearning making me want nothing more than to rip off my pants and bury my cock deep inside of her tight, swollen figure. But I couldn't—not tonight—not without my brother. We'd already done too much apart and I wasn't about to exacerbate the divide. Stacey and I would have a little fun. We were owed that much. But anything more should be shared between the three of us, as was right between perfect pairs.

Stacey's belly was too beautiful for words, and even though part of me was jealous, all I could be in this moment was happy. I felt grateful for the chance to be here with my mate. This was our opportunity to develop a connection with which we could grow together, to function smoothly as a delicious unit of three.

She opened her legs wider in invitation.

Without hesitation, I slid my fingers into her pussy, groaning as her tight, warm flesh gripped me hard. "Oh, fuck, you're so perfect," I whispered against her lips.

"I need you, please," she whispered back. "David, I want you."

I added a second finger and thrust inside her, deeper and deeper, over and over.

Her hips rocked against my hand, riding my fingers toward her bliss. "Oh... David... *please*... I..."

"Come on, Stacey," I growled, kissing her neck, and whispering to her how perfect she was. "Come for me, my beautiful girl."

Her pussy squeezed tightly as she continued to grind into my hand soundlessly, her expression pensive. Then a gasp caught in her throat, and her whole body tensed.

Oh, damn... she is so beautiful.

Her cry as it tore from her lips was the sweetest thing I'd ever heard, and she clung to me desperately as she came in my arms.

In that moment, I knew what it felt like to be truly happy. She was my mate—*our mate*—and I knew it beyond a shadow of a doubt. I may not have been there at the start, but I was a part of it now, and I'd be here for her and my brother until the end.

When she stopped shivering in pleasure, her eyes opened in wonder, and she stared up at me. "That was amazing."

"It was," I agreed, withdrawing my hand from her sinfully gorgeous body, and kissing her tight, dusky pink nipple one more time.

"Aren't you going to take your pants off?" she asked, her eyes alight with desire and an excitement that had me wishing I didn't care about my brother, or our throuple bonding.

She wanted me, and if I stripped off now, I could roll her over and she'd open her legs for me willingly and welcome me into her body. The thought made me shudder with the strength it took to push back against my own needs. I lifted my head and stared down at her with complete adoration. "You know how much I want you, don't you?"

She smiled sensually as she reached down and caressed the bulge of my pants, my cock hard and straining against the fabric, eager for release.

Her soft touch had me groaning, but I bit down hard to lock my jaw and hold firmly to my resolve. "Obviously," I said, through gritted teeth. "And although I'd love nothing more than to fuck your sweet, sweet body until we were both spent, we can't. Not tonight, I'm sorry, beautiful."

Her lips parted with a gasp. "Oh…"

I dropped my head and kissed her again. "You know I want you. But if we're going to be a family—Tommy, you and me—I can't. Not tonight."

Her hands went to her belly, "But Tommy and I already…" she began to reason, so desperate in her need.

Yeah, I know you did.

I sighed. Though her desire was flattering, my erection was already beginning to die. "I know. But I want to do this right, moving forward. Okay?" I slid off the bed and got to my feet, even though I was beginning to hate myself *and* my brother.

I deserve a fucking Brother of the Year Award for this.

Stacey came along with me, then smoothly dropped to her knees before me, her big eyes doe-like and full of emotion.

I stared down at her, not quite comprehending.

Oh, God. She's not going to beg, is she? Because I can't make it through that.

"What are you doing?" I asked, my cock beginning to swell once more with a second wind.

"If we can't have sex, can I at least..." She reached out for me, flicking the button of my pants through its hole and tugging eagerly at the zipper.

I stumbled forward, into her waiting hands and her hot, wet mouth. "Are you sure about this?" I asked her, tugging her hair so that she'd be forced to look up at me.

When she did, her breathtaking eyes blazed with a ready and needful heat. "Yes, I am. Your cock is beautiful. Please let me suck it, David. I want to. I need to."

My jaw dropped at her language, at her raw and wanton hunger.

This is what dreams are made of. I would have waited two life-times over just for this moment.

Her hand moved over my stiffening flesh, gripping and stroking me to a painfully full erection. Then she dropped her head once more and took me into her beautiful, lush mouth.

"Oh... wow..." I threw my head back and tangled my fingers in her blonde hair, turned on beyond belief by the erotic and honest nature of what we were sharing.

She sucked my cock deep into her mouth. The pressure was perfect, the heat and wetness of her mouth a vortex of pure plea-sure from whence I never wanted to return. Stacey gripped my shaft, squeezing tightly as she milked me up and down as her lips formed a tight O around my hardness.

I wanted it to last forever, to feel the heat and pleasure go on and on, but my mate was just too damn good at sucking my cock. The mere thought of how incredible she was, and that I'd finally found the woman whom I could love for the rest of my life, had me racing toward the peak of my release. There was no holding back, not this time. I pulled my cock free of her lips. "Shit, baby, I'm going to come."

She grabbed my shaft and pointed it towards her tits, stroking me hard. She stared into my eyes all the while, her beautiful face smiling, willing me to let go.

My balls tightened and my orgasm hit me so fucking hard that my eyes slid closed, as wave after wave of ecstasy flowed over me. Fireworks exploded behind my closed lids, but I forced my eyes open once more to stare down at my mate as I painted her hot, sweat-slick skin with my seed.

She smiled with the most serene look on her face, so at odds with the carnal pleasures we were sharing.

When the aftershocks finally abated, I opened my eyes fully and untangled my fingers from her waterfall of long blonde hair. "Oh my God, Stacey. That was incredible."

She pushed up with her hands and rose from the carpet of the bedroom, her huge belly and plump breasts painted with my glistening cum.

My cheeks heated with a blush as I observed my handiwork. "I think you might need a shower, beautiful. I'm sorry."

She grinned at me. "Don't you dare apologize. That was insanely hot."

I groaned. "You're the one that's hot." Then I took her hand and dragged her into the adjoining bathroom. Together, we shared a quick shower, and though it was fast, I luxuriated in being able to wash her with the pink fluffy loofah and further explore her delicious curves. Then, before I could allow myself to get carried away, I tucked her into bed and pulled my casual kitchen clothes back on. "I have to go, but I'll see you tomorrow, yeah?" I kissed her forehead as her eyes closed, her long, angelic golden hair fanned out over her pillow.

"Yes, please," she sighed, her voice already taking on a satisfied and absent dream-like quality.

I kissed her once more, inhaling her clean, beautiful scent before heading out the door and jogging down the stairs, taking them two at a time, my spirit soaring above the clouds.

Nancy and Wade were in the TV room, grinning at me from the couch as I passed. "Just having a short chat, huh?" they joked with a knowing look.

I saluted them with a grin and left, knowing what I needed to do now. I had a restaurant to close up, then I was heading home to speak to my brother. Together, just as we'd always done, we'd sort out what we were going to do to get ourselves out of this mess and onto a path of healing and unity for our future, our impossibly stunning mate, and *our* beautiful little girl.

Our dreams have finally come true...

CHAPTER 12

TOMMY

I was in bed but not asleep when David finally arrived home. I'd tried to rest, but my brain just wouldn't stop spinning. I heard the front door open, and I got up, sliding on a pair of flannelette pants. Within a minute, there was a knock on my bedroom door. "Coming," I said, opening the door to my brother's back.

He was already walking away toward the kitchen.

So I followed, glad he wanted to talk in a common area.

David was standing with two glasses and our favorite bottle of whiskey in the dining room, his expression a mix of fleeting emotions. "We need to talk," he said.

I reached out and accepted the half-filled tumbler from him gratefully. I needed a stiff drink for what was coming, I could feel it. Something was up, and things were about to get serious. "Yeah. We do," I agreed.

David tossed back his entire drink, sculling the whiskey, and wincing as the alcohol burned down his throat. "I want Stacey too," he managed in the aftermath, his gaze intense as fuck.

My eyebrows flicked upwards.

Holy shit!

That wasn't what I'd expected him to say. "Ah... yeah, of course. I assumed you would when you came to your senses." My gut twisted with the thought, even though I should have been ready for him to feel this way. I'd always known we'd share our mate, but I couldn't deny the secret joy that had sprung from Stacey being *all* mine, even just for a little while.

"It fucking hurt that you found her and slept with her without me," my brother admitted. "I don't want to sound like a damn pussy, but it did. I hated the idea that you just stormed ahead into your new life without me. We were meant to be a family. You and me and our mate. It was always supposed to be something we did together, not separately."

I swallowed hard, very conscious that I could not screw up this moment. My twin was being real, and he needed my reassurance, not my petty jealousy. "I didn't know at the time, David. I swear it. If I had known, or had any inkling? I would have put her on a plane with me and brought her straight home—for both of us. I know I should have recognized the signs, but I was wasted. The *zing* all of it just went over my head. Back at the conference, she was just another woman. The most beautiful one I'd ever been with, but no different than any other."

I'd never wanted to get married or have a life different from the one David and I had always planned. "It wasn't intentional, I swear," I said. "You have to believe me. Not meeting her, sleeping with her, or getting her pregnant. And if I'd known she was destined to be mine, I would never have let her go in the first place."

"She's *not* just yours," my twin corrected. "She's my mate too, so we should all bond together," David said, his tone terse and annoyed at my misstep.

"I agree."

There was a heavy beat of silence that fell between us.

Where is this conversation headed now?

"I went to see Stacey tonight. At Wade and Tanner's new place," my brother said, shattering the awkward silence like a hammer through glass.

My jaw tightened as my teeth clenched. I couldn't help the way my body reacted. "When?" I prompted.

David shrugged. "I don't know, an hour or two ago, maybe? It doesn't matter."

"What did you do with her?" I asked, inhaling deeply. My brother smelled of sweat and soap, and the normal level of kitchen grease he brought home with him each night. I couldn't smell my—*our*— mate... but that didn't necessarily mean anything.

David shrugged again, his gaze sliding to the floor. "Does it really matter?"

I inhaled sharply again. "It shouldn't," I answered. My brother had every right to sleep with Stacey, and I shouldn't care. But I did, which was fucking stupid! How I felt went against everything I knew about how this was supposed to work. It made no sense.

David chuckled, breaking the tension between us. "We suck at this, you know? Why did we ever think that we could share a woman?" he asked, shaking his head.

My ribs squeezed tightly, making my heart pound a little harder. "Because we're a perfect pair! This is our fate, brother," I emphasized. "It always has been."

David poured himself another generous serving of whiskey and took another sip with a grimace. "And yet, here we are, both jealous assholes. Like toddlers unable to share a toy."

I took another slug of my own whiskey, and it burned hotly down my throat, proving a great distraction from the strange trembling in my heart. "You believe me, don't you? That I didn't know Stacey was my mate when I met her, right?"

David stared at me. "How is that even possible? I mean, I know you say you were wasted, but..."

I groaned, annoyed at my own weakness and stupidity. "I was *blind* drunk. It's a miracle I remember any of the conference at all after how much I had, honestly. And Stacey and I fell into bed within minutes of meeting each other. All I could think at the time was that she was the most beautiful woman I'd ever seen. But that was it, at the time. Then, the next morning, she was gone."

David grabbed the bottle, clearly ready to drown his sorrows, and lumbered over to the small couch area, then flopped down with a sigh. "Yeah, I'd wondered about that part. You know, you missing all the signs. You must have been really fucked up, brother. I only wish I'd been there to meet her too. Maybe I might have realized for the both of us."

I followed after him and sat in the black leather armchair, throwing the rest of my whiskey back and hissing at the sting. "Yeah, me too. That would have been a hell of a lot easier than all of this."

We sat there for a moment in a quiet state of tentative peace. But I had to know what had happened between Stacey and David. Even though it made no sense for me to continue to feel jealous... *I'd* already not only had sex with Stacey, but gotten her pregnant to boot, so if David had *sealed the deal* tonight, so to speak, how could I even dare complain?

I want us to be a throuple, don't I?

"I didn't mate with her tonight," David said suddenly as if reading my mind. "I wanted to, but I didn't."

Well, he'd evidently done something with her, that much was obvious. But now, the "what" wasn't the question I wanted to ask anymore. What I really needed to know was— "Why not?" I asked, my brow furrowed.

David sighed deeply and leaned back against the couch cushions. "Because it felt wrong. We're meant to be a family, Tommy, and you might not have known she was our mate when you met her, but I do *now*. She's mine, she's yours, she's ours. And that should be celebrated, together. We need to do this right for our girls and for our future moving forward."

I smiled as I leaned forward and grabbed the bottle he was nursing, sloshing more amber liquid into our glasses. "I couldn't have said it better myself, brother."

David stared at me for a long, intense minute. "We found her, Tommy. We've got her. Finally. Now. Already, and I... can't believe it. We've been wanting this woman our whole lives and suddenly, she's just here." He shook his head in wonder.

I couldn't help but smile. It was a truly astounding time in our lives.

We continued to drink in silence for a while, enjoying the comfort of knowing that we'd found the woman we'd waited decades for. That needed to be celebrated. My brother was right. Hell, if I had my way I'd shout it from the rooftops. But there was more to deal with here than just the normal mating rituals. We had a baby on the way, and that would create a whole new dynamic and set of obstacles to overcome.

"I want to buy a bigger house," I said, needing to voice my concerns for the future. "Closer to Mom and Dad, maybe?"

Though, I didn't want to be *too* close to them. Everywhere in town was practically ten minutes away from everything else, anyway, so we didn't need to be living on their doorstep, but a bit closer for the sake of support and babysitting assistance would be amazing.

David nodded slowly, the cogs of his mind starting to spin, and he thought of something. "You know, I noticed there's one for sale a few doors down from Wade and Tanner's new place," he suggested casually.

I grinned. "Not *too* close to Mom and Dad then."

David grinned, an amused glint in his dark eyes. "But close enough for babysitting, huh?"

I groaned. "Yeah, God. Babysitting. We're going to need it. I can't believe I'm going to be a father."

David made a wounded sound upon hearing my words.

It had me instantly regretting my turn of phrase. "Shit. Sorry, man. I didn't mean..."

"Yes, you did," he corrected. "I get it. And I don't want you to think that I'm trying to steal your thunder or anything, but if we're going to try and make this family thing work..."

"Then Stacey's baby is *ours*," I said, feeling more resolute in my words now. "That's how it is with perfect pairs. It has to be or there are going to be issues."

David nodded, his jaw tight. "I'm not saying I won't be jealous that this baby's genetically yours, but if you and Stacey still want me to join the family...?"

"We do!" I said. "Well, I know *I* do. And from what you've said, Stacey wants you too." I was damn certain that David and I wouldn't even be having this discussion if he wasn't more solid about Stacey's feelings than a maybe.

David nodded. "Yeah, she doesn't quite understand it yet, and we still haven't told her that we're shifters, and that's a bridge we're going to have to cross at some point—but I believe she wants me too."

I stared at him for a moment, then shook my head as my eyes widened. "Fuck. I didn't even think of that."

He coughed out half a laugh. "That's because we don't view it as weird. It's just our life. But humans do. Tanner told me some time ago that Nancy freaked out when she finally found out."

Damn... more potential unrest. Crap.

"Well, we have to tell her. She's going to see us shift or something soon enough."

"Yep, she is. And our relationship will be better without us keeping secrets from her," David said, refilling our glasses again.

I was beginning to feel the warm and fuzzy feeling you got when alcohol began to saturate your veins. It was relaxing after such a tumultuous start to our throuple relationship. "So, what's the plan, then? Get a house, tell her we're wolves, then fuck her brains out until we're well and truly mated, so she never wants to leave us?"

David held up his glass in a silent toast. "Not necessarily in that order, but yes," he agreed heartily.

I laughed and threw my head back against the headrest, closing my eyes. "A week ago, I thought our mate would never find us. Now, we've got a baby due in three months, a new car, and a house to buy. We're running late, and we didn't even know we were in the race!"

David stood up, drawing my attention.

I opened my eyes and looked up to meet his glassy gaze.

"I'm going to bed," he announced with a yawn.

I nodded. "No problem. Are we good, bro?"

David smiled. "Yeah, brother. We're good. We always will be. But you owe me, you know that? When we take Stacey to bed next, I get to make love to her first."

I didn't like that idea, and neither did my wolf.

Ugh. Stupid fucking jealousy!

But I nodded. I had to. It was only fair. "Okay," I agreed. I'd already been inside Stacey's incredible body, and it wouldn't be long before I felt the velvety clasp of her pussy around my cock once more. I just had to be patient.

"Night," David said, saluting me as he walked past me and back toward the stairs again.

I stayed downstairs for a while, mulling over the next steps we needed to take. We had more than enough money between us, but we both worked way too much. That would have to change. Could I scale back my hours or could David perhaps hire another head chef to take his shifts some nights? How was this going to work in a practical, real way. Our current place was modern and minimalist. Not good for a baby or a woman with a heart like sunshine.

We absolutely needed a new house and we had to be honest with our mate about who and *what* we were. David was right yet again. A secret like that could prove toxic to our chances of a future together if we didn't get upfront about it real soon.

It can't go too badly, surely?

She'd taken everything in stride so far, and Nancy and Lexie had gotten over the shifter issue successfully as far as I knew. No doubt Stacey would be good with our true identities in no time.

Right? She has to be...

CHAPTER 13

STACEY

I woke up with my belly cramping, and not from hunger. "Ow," I moaned as I gripped my baby bump and forced myself to take some slow, steady breaths. "No, please no!" *I can't be in labor. She isn't ready yet.*

I lay perfectly still, hoping and praying for the pain to go away. Despite my best efforts to remain calm and soothe my body, the cramps only increased in their severity. I cried out, rolling over and reaching out for my phone. I punched the screen to find Tommy's number and pushed call. My breath shuddered out of me as I focused on keeping myself calm.

"Good morning beautiful," Tommy's smooth voice flowed through the phone. "How'd you sleep?"

But there was no time for pleasantries. Not now. "I'm cramping," I blurted, unable to hide my fear. "I'm scared." Another groan of pain tore from my lips and my brows furrowed deeply as I grimaced through the uncomfortable sensation. "I don't know what's happening."

"Stay there. We're coming," Tommy answered and hung up.

I threw the phone across my bed to sob in fear. What would

this mean for us if the baby came now? Would she survive at just twenty-six weeks? Could she?

My door flew open, and Nancy ran in, dropping to her knees beside my bed. "Are you okay? What's happened? Tommy just called me. The boys are on their way here with the ambulance."

"I'm cramping," I whispered, hot tears spilling over my cheeks as my baby rolled and kicked, causing another painful wave of spasms. "I think I'm in labor," I sobbed.

Nancy held my hand until the ambulance arrived, for which I was eternally grateful. I felt so alone and frightened.

Thankfully, Tommy was what seemed like mere moments behind them. He assessed me—found that I wasn't bleeding—but advised I go straight to the hospital, regardless. He swung me up in his arms like a real-life hero and carried me down the stairs. How he did that with my current weight, I'll never know. But in the sea of uncertainty and pain, Tommy was there, kissing my head and promising me that everything was going to be okay.

I traveled in the ambulance with the two paramedics, while Tommy followed in his own vehicle behind us.

"Dr. Bailey is a great doctor," one of the paramedics said.

I gasped and groaned as another wave of contractions hit me without mercy. "I have no doubt, but he's not my doctor. He's the father." I'm sure the female paramedic reacted to my news, but I was too invested in what was going on inside my belly to notice. My entire world had narrowed down to my body and the little life that was kicking up a storm far too early for comfort.

They wheeled me inside on a gurney and David was there waiting for me, pacing the entrance with a look of stoic concern on his face. He came straight over and grabbed my hand as they pushed me into a sterile white room.

"David, I'm scared," I whispered to him, my voice shaky and my heart in my throat. "I can't lose her." Tears silently spilled down my cheeks, dampening my hairline, betraying just how petrified I was.

He gripped my hand tight and stared down at me, his dark eyes intense but steady in the sea of drama. "I've got you," he promised. "And you won't. Don't even think that. We won't let it happen."

The ER doctors gave me some drugs to slow down or hopefully stop the contractions altogether. Then they followed up with an ultrasound and some bloodwork, before committing me to bed rest until further notice.

David stayed with me for hours, just holding my hand. And although he said very little, his presence comforted me in ways no words could have.

"Hey," Tommy said, walking into my room unexpectedly, brandishing a clipboard. "How are you feeling, Stacey?"

I wriggled carefully to sit up higher in bed before I cradled my belly with both hands. I ignored his question. It was the least of my concerns. I only cared about our baby, our little girl. "What's happening?" I asked. "Is the baby okay?"

"She's doing fine," Tommy assured me with a smile. "The pre-term labor has stopped for now, but you'll be on bed rest from now until the birth, I'm afraid."

Oh, God...

I blanched at the thought, and my mind whirled with panic. "But I don't even have any insurance," I protested. "I can't stay here! I'll be in debt until I die!"

"You won't stay here, you'll come home with us. And don't even worry about the money. We told you, it's taken care of," David said firmly.

I bit my lip, my heart still racing.

Taken care of? How?

"David's right," Tommy added. "We can take you home as early as tomorrow, but I think it's best you stay in here overnight.

I'll arrange for an OBGYN friend to come here later this week to assess you. But either way, our place is only a two-minute drive, so if anything happens at all, we can come straight back in no time flat."

"Will the baby survive if she comes out now?" I asked, my throat tightening under the stress of asking such a question. There were many fears a pregnant woman carried with her for the nine months her baby relied on her, and having a premature birth was definitely chief among them.

Tommy sat on the bed and touched my leg, offering me his sense of physical calm. "She's staying in there for now, so try to relax. There's nothing in your bloodwork or ultrasound that leads me to believe this is anything more than a sign that you need to rest. You've been all over the place looking for the father of your baby, with little thought for your own wellbeing. That mentality has to stop. Your health is just as important as the baby's. We'll going to take care of you, okay? You have our word."

I nodded, but I knew what he was really saying. If the baby came now, she might not make it, or at the very least, she'd be fighting for each and every breath she took, and I didn't want that for her. "I'll do anything you say to make sure she stays healthy and safe," I declared without hesitation.

"I'm glad," Tommy said as he stood up and came over to kiss me on the forehead. It was a strange but sweet gesture. "You get some rest, and I'm going to make some phone calls." Then he took his leave, nodding to his brother as he did.

David stayed with me until dinnertime, then he kissed my lips tenderly. "I'm going to set up the dinner shift over at the restaurant, then get the house ready for your arrival. I'll pop by later to say goodnight, then I'll pick you up tomorrow, okay?"

I gripped his hand, hard. I wanted him to know just how much I needed him. "We're okay, aren't we? I mean, you and me? Us?"

He reached out and spread his hand protectively over my baby bump in the most beautiful gesture of partner and family solidarity I'd ever witnessed, and my heart melted inside me at the sight. The baby kicked hard in response to his touch, and David's eyes widened, a small smile gracing his lips "Of course, we're all okay, Stacey. We'll get through this together, okay?"

I nodded, but I still felt more than a little uneasy. This was my first pregnancy and I never thought I'd turn out like this. "Okay," I breathed, giving him what I hoped was a brave face.

David went to leave, pausing to watch me from the door for a moment before he shook his head as if at himself, and disappeared down the hall.

The nurses on shift fussed over me for the rest of the night and into the next morning. I'd never really stayed in a hospital before, though I'd heard plenty of stories about them not being that nice. But the food I was given wasn't too terrible, and my bed was comfortable. Given I was receiving around the clock care —no doubt thanks to Tommy's influence—what more could I ask for? I was just grateful our little one was all right for the moment.

The boys must have made alternative arrangements, because instead of David, it was Tommy who came by to pick me up at around lunchtime. I had nothing to wear so he took me straight to a dress shop in town and Tommy racked up a huge balance for too many clothes in record time. "You don't need the stress," he said. "You just point, and we'll take it home."

And even though I'd done next to nothing other than exactly that, by the time he got me home, I was exhausted.

Tommy took me by the arm and walked me into their beautiful townhouse.

Its modern lines and monochromatic color palette made me smile. It was so masculine, it bordered on being clinical. "Your home is beautiful," I said as I plodded along slowly, relying on my mate's strength.

Tommy led me through the small living room and toward a bedroom. "I've moved all of my stuff into the spare bedroom so that you can have my bed," he said. "And before you refuse to accept it, my bedroom is the only one in the house with an ensuite, and you'll need to be close to a bathroom."

I stared up at him with literal stars in my eyes. "How did I get so lucky as to have you?"

Tommy jolted and stared at me, then laughed. "Oh, sweetheart, I love hearing you say that, but you have *no* idea how long I've waited for you. How long we've waited for you."

I shuffled the rest of the way into the bedroom to find warmer wooden tones and a palette of fawns and browns.

"Thank you," I said. "This is lovely. I'm just so sorry for being such a pain."

He chuckled. "You're not. Far from it, beautiful. You're perfect. Besides, now we get to spoil you, and you won't run away from us."

I laughed as I kicked off my shoes, tossed back the duvet, and rolled onto the huge king-sized bed. There, in absolute bliss, I collapsed onto the fluffy pillows. "I'm not going anywhere."

"Perfect. Now, do you want lunch or a nap first?"

I closed my eyes and let out a tired sigh. "I think I'll pass out right here. Food is going to have to wait."

He leaned over and kissed my forehead again, which was nice but was kind of annoying to.

What's up with that?

"Can I have a real kiss?" I asked, forcing my eyes open to meet his.

His eyes went wide, then the blue diamonds of his gaze sparkled. "Of course." But instead of the passionate kiss I'd been hoping for, he pressed his lips gently to mine in a tender, but chaste kiss. He pulled back with a smile. "Now get some sleep. I have to pop into the clinic for a while, but David will be home soon. We've moved shifts around as much as we can this week, but we'll be out a bit still. I'm sorry. Short notice and all, but next week will be better."

I pulled the duvet up closer to my chin, feeling warm and safe for the first time in a long time. "Thank you, Tommy, for keeping me and the baby safe. I'll never forget this."

He kissed my cheek this time and lingered to whisper in my ear. "That's what I'm here for, beautiful girl. Now, rest. There's food in the fridge, and I'm only a three-minute drive away if you need me. You only have to call."

I smiled and nodded my thanks as he left. Everything went quiet and our baby girl shifted inside of me. I couldn't help but smile. I'd been so afraid yesterday—of losing her—of losing everything. But now I was safe, and so was she. Tommy might be leaving for work, but David would be home soon. And regardless of where either of them was at any given moment in time, I knew we had each other, and that they'd take care of me.

I think I'm really starting to believe it.

After so long a journey and a little more pain than my fair share, things were finally working out. And with that thought in mind, peace stole over me, and I allowed my eyes to close and gave in to the alluring promise of sleep.

CHAPTER 14

STACEY

The next month just flew by. Between specialist appointments, including scans, and regular baby measurements—due in part not just because of my premature labor scare, but also my significant weight loss, not to mention a ton of movies and sleep—I was solidly occupied despite being put on strict bed rest. The boys made sure that someone was with me most of the time, so between them, Nancy, and Lexie, I always had someone to keep me company.

Our daughter was growing well, proving herself to be a tough little girl, and we'd officially hit thirty weeks. The elation I felt knowing that our baby had immensely better odds of survival if she was born now was immense. Her lungs were developing quickly, preparing her for the world beyond my womb, and thanks to the OB/GYN I'd seen this morning, I was looking forward to my evening.

"What do you want for dinner?" Tommy asked when he arrived home after his day shift. "I was thinking... steak maybe?"

I grinned at him from my comfy little nest on the couch. "Sounds perfect." The boys cooked a lot of meat. They almost ate like freaking carnivores and had the appetites to boot, but considering my low iron levels, I was grateful. I turned toward the kitchen with one thing on my mind.

Tommy was busy pulling out potatoes and various fresh salad ingredients.

I licked my lips and cleared my throat. "So, do you think we could maybe spend some time together tonight?" I asked.

His dark gaze flicked up to meet mine, his brows furrowed. "Don't we always?"

"David is coming home tonight too, yeah?" It was a rare evening when they were both home and I was still awake.

Tommy nodded. "Yeah, why? You got something special planned?" he ventured.

Butterflies flicked their wings up inside my belly as I slowly smiled at him. "Yes. Yes I do, as a matter of fact."

It had been *too* long since we'd been intimate. The boys routinely took turns sleeping beside me in bed, and while they were affectionate and loving, neither of them had done more than give me a chaste kiss on the lips in the past month, and it was driving me crazy.

Especially David.

I sighed. He was kind as always, but there was something about the way he held himself in control all the time that reminded me of a caged lion. There was restrained power there, and I so, so, *so* wanted to see him unleashed and allowed to go wild.

David arrived home half an hour later, and we ate our delicious, fresh meal together.

I was practically bouncing with energy after an earlier nap during the day, but I also knew that my energy was limited and struck infrequently, so I needed to act quickly and seize this precious opportunity before it faded, and I was relegated to another night of sweet snuggles.

David was talking about work and their extended family at length, but as soon as he stopped to take a breath, I jumped in, seizing the night as it were.

"Can you both sleep with me tonight?" I asked, waiting with bated breath for their response.

Tommy and David shared a worried look, then turned toward me, unspeaking.

"Is it my size?" I asked when the silence dragged on, putting my hands around my huge belly defensively. "Are you both repulsed by me now?" Thanks to the "no stress" lifestyle, couch time, and likely *too much* food, I'd put on a stack of weight. I had the big belly, of course, but now my boobs and ass were having a competition as to who could get biggest, fastest.

"No, no of course not," Tommy said, reaching under the table to touch my leg affectionately. "We just... well, we agreed. We're trying to keep you and the baby as safe as possible until the birth and even then, you'll need a reasonable amount of time to heal. And to be honest, we're worried that putting us all together will just encourage—"

"Good!" I interjected, my hope returning. "Dr. Mayer told me this morning I'm healthy as can be, and I can go back to regular, everyday duties as well if I want. Cooking, cleaning... *sex*."

David coughed to clear out his throat. "We've already got a cleaner, sweetheart. And I like to cook for us."

I grinned at him. "Then sex it is! If you guys want to, that is?" My gaze flicked hungrily between the two brothers, and I could see their fear. "What's worrying you two so much? The pregnancy? Like Dr. Mayer said—I'm okay now. You can stop freaking out. I'm not made of glass."

David nodded. "Yeah, well, you went into hospital after we were together the night before, and I just didn't want that happening again. Not on my account. I could never forgive myself if something happened, Stacey."

"Dr. Mayer said that wasn't because we'd been intimate, it was just a culmination of the stress due to the months before. All the fear, the traveling, the uncertainty before I found you both. But everything's amazing now, I promise." I stared at them, watching as they battled their desires, or at least that's what I hoped the fleeting emotions dancing across their faces were.

Nancy had told me earlier today that if I wanted the boys to take me to bed, then I'd have to step out of my comfort zone and use my words. I'd have to be more forward than I was used to being, because communication in a ménage was key. I swallowed, remembering her advice and pushed my own fear down. I'd been positively *aching* for them for weeks now, and my body's needs were climbing higher with every day of good health to the point of desperation.

"I want you," I managed to say. "My body needs you. And I know I'm not the prettiest I've ever been, but if you want me at all, I'd love it if we could—"

David stood up and held out his hand to me, his eyes blazing. "Let's go."

I blinked up at him. His voice had turned deep and gravelly. "Really?" I asked, almost afraid to hope that he'd agreed so quickly to my desires.

He nodded, the tension in his body obvious with the tightening of his jaw and the slight shaking of his hand.

"Oh, thank you!" I said, taking his hand and letting him pull me to my feet.

We didn't go straight to the bedroom like I'd thought we would. Instead, he gripped my face in both hands and kissed me hard, right then and there near the dinner table.

And just like that, I was lost in his passion, in his seeking tone and moans of pleasure. I grabbed at his shirt, holding on tight while I rode the wave. I was finally getting what I wanted and what I'd spent so long fearing and second-guessing. But now that it was here and happening, I couldn't fathom how I'd ever thought this union of our flesh as a threesome could be anything but wonderful.

Tommy's hands slid around my waist, his body pressing into me from behind.

I gasped and moaned at the intensity of the sensations, gripping tighter when I sensed David trying to pull away. "No, please don't go!" I panicked. "I want both of you... at the same time," I admitted bravely, my voice sultrier than I could have ever planned for.

He practically growled in response. "Come to the bed so I can feel you."

I went with him all too willingly, just overwhelmed and grateful for this chance to be with both the men I loved.

Tommy's hands were on me as we moved into the bedroom I'd spent the last month occupying. The sheets were pink now, and Tommy had bought me a new floral duvet as well. He'd said the color and bright nature theme suited me more, because I was the sunshine in their life, and I couldn't have been more touched by the sweet and thoughtful gesture.

David threw back the covers, and together they worked in tandem to relieve me of my clothes. Between passionate kisses and lingering, exploratory touches, my new maternity clothes fell away, piling up on the floor, and I was left naked as the day I was born.

David stared at me, his expression that of a hungry predator. It frightened me and turned me on all at once. I was catching a glimpse of that caged lion.

I lifted my hands to cover my breasts, a flush of shame and anxiety racing through me in the moment. "I know, I'm really big now," I apologized.

He reached out and dragged my hands down, exposing my huge boobs, my previously pinkish nipples now a darker shade of rose and tight with need of him. "You're perfect. I like you better like this," he said with shockingly delicious honesty. "You look like a goddess. Like dreams come to life."

Tommy's hands slid around from behind me in ready agreement, cupping both breasts and squeezing my nipples tenderly between his forefingers and thumbs.

I cried out with desire. "Please get naked," I begged, pulling at David's shirt as he stood in front of me. "I need to touch you."

David whipped off his shirt and unzipped his pants, letting them fall to the floor without a single word.

I stepped forward, eagerly wrapping my hand around his already thickened cock.

He groaned, his eyes closing for a moment as I worked him, his hand slipping between my thighs.

Tommy's lips were on my neck, peppering my skin with slow, protective kisses as he savored the taste of my flesh.

I turned my head to kiss him, to include him in the all-encompassing passion I was feeling assaulting my ready body.

David's fingers flicked over my clit, teasing me, clearly enjoying the way I pressed into his wicked ministrations.

I gasped and groaned in pleasure as tendrils of heat rose and coiled, tightening deep within my core. Opening my thighs further, I gave him unhindered access to my body.

Tommy lifted his head from my neck, his eyes glazed with lust. "Would being on your knees be the most comfortable for you?" he whispered, his breath hot against my ear.

My head was fuzzy as I continued to lose myself to my men, but I had to answer the question. I had to maintain communication and be brave. I had to tell them what I wanted.

Positions with this belly...

"Yes, that would be the best, I think," I scarcely managed by sheer force of will.

David guided me to the edge of the bed, cornering me against it and gently pushed me down. "I need to be inside you, Stacey," he said. "Don't make me wait any longer, beautiful."

I turned around and climbed onto the mattress and knelt, going down onto my forearms so my belly rested on the bed. "I need to feel you inside me too." Without further instruction, I spread my legs wide and tilted my pelvis back for him, displaying myself to my mate like a female in heat.

David stepped up behind me, rubbing the head of his gleaming cock up and down the seam of my juicy pussy.

With a needy whimper, I pushed back, wanting him inside me *now*.

Oh, God. This is happening! It's really happening.

Tommy slid across the bed in front of me, settling on his knees, and offered me his cock to suck.

Fuck, yes!

My mind almost imploded with the sheer sexiness of what we were sharing. I couldn't say no. I didn't fucking want to! I couldn't imagine anything more amazings than taking his cock deep inside my throat as his brother filled me from behind. It would be the most erotic thing I'd ever done in my life.

I grabbed his cock with my hand readily and held it tightly. He was longer and thicker than I remembered, and he'd never looked more delicious. I moaned in ecstasy as I wrapped my lips around him, tasting the saltiness of his skin, reveling in the glorious way he felt both hard and soft at the same time.

David's hands gripped my hips firmly as he readied himself for what we'd both been waiting for.

I gasped around Tommy's cock as I felt his brother press into me.

David thrust slowly into my pussy, taking his sweet time as he extracted every possible iota of pleasure from our union. Inch by inch, he impaled me on his perfect, thick cock.

The further he forged within me, the more I wanted. And

when I finally felt him sink balls deep, I drove myself back, grinding against him and crying out at the pleasure ramping up inside me.

He began to move, pumping into me over and over with wild abandon, driving away any and all doubts and worries I might have ever had. With his carnal love, he banished all the nights I'd spent sleeping beside them, worrying that they didn't want me in return. Fearing that they didn't desire me and would never love me.

How stupid I've been!

As my belly tightened and my pussy quivered uncontrollably while my boys' two cocks plunged reverently and enthusiastically inside my body, I realized with startling clarity I'd never been happier.

O, my God! Fuck!

My orgasm hit me hard and fast, almost driving the breath from my lungs with brutal force. My pussy convulsed, and wave after wave of hot, shuddering pleasure crashed over me. Without an ounce of regret or shame, I screamed around Tommy's cock, unable to control the rampant chaos seizing my body from within.

He tried to pull away, intent on removing himself from my mouth and finishing on his own chest and belly.

But I wasn't having any of that. I grasped him firmly, jacking him off as I bobbed my head, eager to have both of my boys finish inside me. A few wickedly intense moments later I felt Tommy's hot load explode at the back of my throat. With a concerted effort I swallowed him down, unwilling to spill a single drop.

Tommy's cursing filled the air as he bucked and shivered in the aftermath of his release, falling backward onto the pillows, clearly stunned by my enthusiasm and prowess.

David began to move harder and faster then, shattering my

reality as he pushed me even higher toward a level of bliss I'd never experienced before. He made sparkling lights flash and dance behind my eyelids until I couldn't take it a second longer, and I came again.

This time I shook like a leaf in the wind, unable and entirely unwilling to stop the animal-like noises that fell from my lips and tore from my throat.

David thrust once more inside me, his pelvis slamming into my ass, then he stiffened and came too. The hot pulses of his seed caressed my insides as his hands dug possessively into my hips and he cried out.

His cry of completion was *so* unbelievably wild and hot that I bit into the sheets beneath my face as I rode the last shreds of my pleasure, shivering under the intense and beautiful duress of my own completion.

We fell together toward the bed, rolling carefully to the side to protect my belly.

Soon after, Tommy did a quick check on me and the baby, just to make sure we hadn't shaken things up too much. But once we both passed his tests, still panting and sweaty, we lay together, all three of us.

We were together at last, and cradled safely between my perfect pair, I'd never felt more sated or happy.

CHAPTER 15

DAVID

I was the first to wake up the next morning following our throuple union, but I didn't dare move in case I woke up my twin and my mate. Stacey's head was on the same pillow as mine, and when I opened my eyes, I could see her beautiful face right there in front of me. Her luscious lips were pink and parted as she softly snored, and her eyelashes fluttered ever so slightly as she dreamed.

I ached to reach out and cup her cheek to tell her how much I adored her and how grateful I was that she had finally come into our life. But I didn't. Such declarations of love could wait for a more opportune moment. Instead, I chose not to interrupt her and simply let her sleep. Watching her, emotions I'd never felt before cascaded over me, making me feel whole for the first time in living memory.

Tommy's head popped up from behind Stacey's halo of golden blonde hair, and my brother smiled in a way I'd never seen him before. He wore a satisfied and happy expression that told me he was feeling exactly the same way I was this morning —completely fulfilled.

Stacey began to stir and rolled onto her back, groaning softly as though in pain, then her eyes fluttered open and she smiled. "Good morning, boys."

"How are you feeling?" I asked quickly, sliding my hand over her swollen belly, loving the feel of her warm flesh shifting and moving as our child rolled and kicked from within.

"Great," Stacey said brightly, then groaned. "Though our little girl sure is getting too strong for my ribs."

A flush of heat filled my face as strong emotions filled my heart to overflowing. I still had brief moments, even now, where my insecurities got the better of me and I feared that Tommy and Stacey would leave me out once their daughter was born. Then came the question that plagued me most...

Should I hold back and remain reserved in case they do?

I wasn't the baby's father, after all. Not until Stacey declared it so, and I hadn't heard those exact words from her mouth just yet. My stomach grumbled loudly with hunger, and I rolled out of bed. "Back soon," I said before going to the bathroom to use the toilet and get cleaned up. When I returned to the bedroom, I was struck with the sudden desire to cook. I needed something hearty and homemade after last night, that was for damn sure. And no one else cooked like me.

"Shall I make French toast this morning, or would you like something else?" I asked, still standing naked in all my glory.

"Oh, yes. French toast please," Stacey said, excitement clear in her voice.

It always pleased me and put my mind at ease when our mate's appetite was strong. It was good for her and the baby. I grinned to myself as I left the bedroom, not sure what they would do in my absence, but to be honest... I didn't care after all what we'd shared last night.

Over the course of our lives together I would have my fair share of alone time with our mate, and Tommy would too. I couldn't continue to be jealous. I had to rein it in as best I could and just go with the flow. Ménages were difficult to navigate at the best of times from what I'd heard, so we'd all just have to be as open and honest as we could be and hope for the best. Besides, I had been the one to come inside Stacey's tight pussy last night, so how could I complain?

My brother hadn't, though Stacey had taken his load down her throat, and I was pretty sure he was happy about that. It was always better when you didn't have to pull out.

I'd prepared most of breakfast when I heard Tommy and Stacey slowly making their way downstairs. When they entered the kitchen, I waved at the table where the trays were filled with syrup and cutlery. "I was going to bring you breakfast in bed," I said.

"Oh, thank you for the thought, but it's *so* good to get out of bed now," Stacey said with a smile. "I know I can't go too far, but even being in the living room is pretty amazing after weeks of only the bedroom walls to stare at."

"Sit then," I said with a smile. "And let's eat."

Stacey ate well, which I was more than happy to see, given her appetite hadn't been that big lately. It was getting to the point where the baby was taking up a lot of real estate, and no doubt her stomach was being compressed inside there. But at least she was smiling and laughing, and there were no signs of another bout of pre-term labor.

"You aren't too sore from last night, are you?" I asked her hopefully, wanting to relieve myself of the last of my lingering guilt.

She shook her head, her cheeks turning rosy. "No, not at all. I feel really great."

I hid my smug smile behind my coffee cup as I took a satisfying sip.

Perfect.

The doorbell rang, and I rose to my feet wearing only the pair of jeans I'd pulled on to do the cooking. When I opened the door expecting to see Mom or Nancy, I was surprised to find a complete stranger on my doorstep.

"Hi," I said, nodding at him, my brow furrowed. "Can I help you?"

In a town our size, I knew practically *everybody*, and this guy didn't look like he was from around here at all. He was tall, but not as tall as me, and he wore an expensive suit with his dark hair slicked back with oil.

The man narrowed his eyes at me. "Yes," he answered curtly. "You can tell me where my wife is."

I laughed at him and crossed my arms over my naked chest, which seemed to infuriate him. "I have no idea who your wife is, stranger. So... I doubt it."

His nostrils flared. "Her name is Stacey Mercer, and I was told she was staying here."

What the fuck!

I swallowed hard, trying not to give this prick the pleasure of seeing me freak out. My entire world began to narrow around me, and panic rose in my chest. I fought it down with a mammoth effort, determined to maintain my poker face.

My mate...

"I'll have to speak to my brother," I said in a tone that offered no room for argument. "Wait here." Turning my back on him, I went to shut the front door.

He slammed his hand against the wood, halting its closure. "She's pregnant," he said, the vehemence in his words like a nail driving through my skull. "And the baby's *mine*. She's *mine*. You get her to come out here, and then I'll be taking her home. Today."

It was my turn to clench my jaw and glare right back at him. "Stacey belongs to no one," I said. "Wait here." I pulled hard, dislodging his arm, then slammed the door in his face with a resounding *thud*. "Fuck!" My chest rose and fell rapidly as I marched back to the kitchen, the dreams for my future seemingly fading with every step I took.

"Who was that?" Tommy asked from behind the island where he was busy putting things away.

"What's wrong?" Stacey asked, getting to her feet, her hands holding her baby belly in her usual protective fashion.

The baby that this asshole, says is his.

"There's a man at our door," I said, trying to stay calm all the while it felt like my blood was boiling inside my veins. "He says that Stacey is his wife, and the baby is *his*."

The happy rosiness of Stacey's cheeks went deathly pale, and her demeanor instantly turned to one of fear. "Jamie's here?" she whispered, her gaze bolting to the front door.

"It's true?" I asked, unable to hide the subtle note of hurt and resentment in my voice.

She shook her head as she sank back down into the chair she'd just been occupying at the dining table. "No!" she gasped. "Well... *yes*, we *were* married. But I left him six months ago! The night I met Tommy."

I gaped at her, trying with all my strength not to be angry, not to be any more hurt by this entire life-shattering situation, but my wolf was already howling inside my mind.

"You got pregnant the night you left your husband?" I asked, just to make sure I understood it right. "How do you know the baby is Tommy's then?"

"Because she is!" Stacey declared, her face stricken as she held her head in her hands.

Tommy walked around the island bench. "Let's just all remain calm. I knew that Stacey had been married previously and had left just before she met me."

"The *night* she met you, Tommy, which means the baby could legitimately be his or ours... right? How do we know?"

Tommy glanced at Stacey. "Well, technically, with the timing... depending on whether she was still sleeping with her ex-husband..."

"I wasn't!" Stacey cried. "And you can't let him see me. Please!"

"Why not?" I asked, not quite understanding her vehement reaction.

"Because I don't want to see him!" she protested, rising from her chair and backing up so that she was soon heading for the back door. "I escaped him once, and I'll never get away again if he gets me to go back home."

She was talking about him like he was abusive. "Did he hurt you?" I pressed, my brow furrowing as my heart continued to gallop in my chest. "What are you trying to say? Just spit it out! We don't have time for this. The prick is right outside."

Her face was red now, and her eyes filled with tears. "I'm saying he's a controlling, manipulative creep! He made sure I never worked so he could control me. He made sure I never had any money of my own at all, so when I left, I was literally starving, homeless, and alone for months!" she cried.

My stomach heaved at the pain and torment in her words.

This is fucked. Completely fucked.

I had just finally come to terms with everything. I'd accepted her, loved her, and her baby, and now this. It was enough to make me sick to my stomach. I turned and stormed back to the front door, wrenching it open. My wolf was so dangerously close to the surface, I was struggling to keep my teeth from shifting.

"Fuck off!" I growled at him. "Your wife isn't here, and if you come here again, you'll be trespassing on private property. We take that *very* seriously around here. We're territorial," I added, letting the unspoken threat hang between us like a burning razor wire.

The asshole lifted his chin indignantly and looked down his nose at me like he was King Shit, and I was some kind of peasant scum. "I tried to do this the cordial way, but if Stacey won't come home of her own volition, I have other ways of forcing her hand. You'll be hearing from my lawyers." He smirked.

A savage growl ripped through my vocal cords, crippled by my rage and doubt, all the while amplified by my pain and frustration.

Stacey's ex, Jamie, jumped back, startled, his eyes wide—the look of surprise on his face breaking his carefully constructed veneer of perfection.

I slammed the door in his face for the second time inside of five minutes just as I lost my fight to my inner wolf and shifted right there and then in the pristine foyer of my damn home. In the place of David the man, stood David the wolf, and he was pissed. Big time.

Well, fuck! That's certainly one way to bring up the shifter conversation...

CHAPTER 16

STACEY

I couldn't believe he'd found me. I couldn't fathom why he'd even come. Jamie was a power-hungry, selfish, abusive, controlling asshole, and I was shaking like a leaf knowing he now knew *exactly* where I was after all these months. "H-he's going to take me," I stuttered to Tommy as he put an arm around my shoulder to prevent my escape toward the back of the house. "I don't know how he found me."

My world had turned upside down in the blink of an eye. One moment I'd been blissfully happy and was finally feeling like I wasn't in a dream, but that I'd actually found my real Nirvana. Now... I was in Hell again. But even worse, my beautiful world was being ripped away from me with each passing second. It didn't escape my notice how upset David looked about all this. Thankfully, Tommy was acting a lot more calm and rational.

"I have to sit down," I breathed, staggering over to the chair at the dining table and dropping into it with a *thump*. The baby was squirming up a storm in my belly—no doubt reacting to my emotions—and my heart was pounding in my chest like I'd just run a fucking marathon.

Who was I kidding? I wasn't running any kind of race, I was in goddamn survival flight mode, Every instinct I possessed screamed at me to make my move before Jamie made his. I needed to get out of here, and fast.

I can't go back. I won't!

I looked up at Tommy. "I need to go. Can you please take me to the train station?"

Tommy sat down and reached out for my hand, his gaze earnest and placating. "Hold on a second, Stacey, take a deep breath. You're not going anywhere."

"I have to!" I said, my growing panic evident in my shrill tone. "Didn't you hear David? Jamie thinks the baby's his, and if he gets hold of me..." I shook my head, unwilling to contemplate the thought any further. "No. I won't go back. I can't."

Jamie was a classic narcissist and an emotional vampire. He'd lured me into the relationship in the beginning with his gorgeous face and sweet promises of true love and a beautiful, luxurious life. But within a few short years I'd found myself isolated from everyone I'd ever known and utterly powerless.

And, of course, it was all my fault. I hadn't run sooner. I'd allowed him to mow me down like clover on the curbside—but I wouldn't let him do it again. I'd learned my lesson the hard way. And while I still had my wits about me and courage left in reserve, I wouldn't go with him. I shook my head again.

No. I won't go back. My daughter will never know what it's like to live with a man like Jamie. I'll make sure of it.

A soft growl that sounded just like a dog's caught my attention. It seemed almost pained or upset... and far too close for comfort.

"Is that coming from inside the house?" I asked, gripping my belly tightly, as though I could save my baby from everything that was going on out here.

"Oh, no," Tommy muttered. "Fuck it! I knew this was going

to happen." He got up and walked over to the doorway that led into the foyer. "You idiot," he admonished.

Who is he talking to? Did David let a dog in the house?

The growling grew louder, and I hefted myself up to my feet and moved behind a chair.

What the hell is going on?

Tommy glanced back at me, his expression apologetic. "Stacey, sweetheart. I'm sorry you had to find out like this. We were waiting to tell you after the birth... when you and the baby were safe and well, but it seems we've missed that chance."

I frowned at him, not comprehending. "I don't know what you're talking about, but I *need* to get out of here. Jamie will come back soon, and he'll bring his lawyers."

Proving emotional abuse and financial control was *so* ridiculously difficult. How could I possibly convince them that I'd been trapped in that toxic marriage and that I hadn't had sex with Jamie for months before I'd left? I'd feigned sickness and thrush and done *other things* to keep him happy. But there was no way he was the father.

No way!

Tommy turned fully toward me. "You're not going anywhere. You're our mate, Stacey, and that's our baby. You can't take her away from us, not now. Please," he begged, pleading to my common sense.

I'd certainly be safer with my boys, but the fact remained that this location was now compromised, and I could be removed by force or the law if it came down to it. My nose burned with emotions, and impending tears pricked at my eyes. "But David said"

"David's an idiot!" Tommy spat.

A warning growl came out from somewhere behind him in response.

"He's an insecure, emotional idiot that loves you, Stacey. Trust me, he doesn't want to lose you any more than I do."

I swallowed hard against the tears. "But he thinks the baby is Jamie's... he won't believe me, and I can't..." I couldn't stay with a man who didn't trust me, who didn't really love me. You couldn't have love without trust and that was a simple, undisputable fact.

"Stacey, listen to me. I love you And David does too. And although I completely trust you when you say that baby is mine, it also doesn't matter to me. I want you and would raise your child as mine, no matter who's it is, anyway. Okay?"

I nodded in sheer disbelief, gulping hard. His declaration was just too heartfelt, and I felt more than unworthy of it. "Okay," I whispered as I swiped at the tears on my cheeks, trying desperately to believe what he was saying. Tommy meant it, I was almost certain. "But David..."

Tommy sighed and shook his head. "David will wrap his head around it, I'm certain. He's just more emotional than me and needs time." He glanced back toward the foyer once more. "Which brings me to the only secret we still have to reveal to you, and you might want to sit down for it."

"But Jamie..." I lifted my hand to indicate that he might come back.

Why is he not taking this seriously? He doesn't know Jamie like I do!

Tommy just smiled, a sinister gleam in his gaze. "Let him try to take you. I'll call our pack and they'll be here in minutes. Hell, Lexie will be on her motorcycle chasing him out of town as soon as she finds out what you've been through."

I took another deep breath, trying to calm the racing of my poor heart. "So, you really won't let him take me? You still want me after all this trouble?"

"Of course not. Fucking hell!" Tommy swore, shaking his head more vehemently this time. "Over my dead body will he touch you ever again," he promised. "And of course we still want you, sweetheart. That will *never* change."

I sank into the chair again, my stomach beginning to calm down from the strange, sickening slithering it had been doing during my near panic attack. "Okay," I breathed. "So, what's this big secret, then?"

Tommy's eyes went dark and sad, and his lips twisted in thought before he began to explain. "Well, you're not going to believe us without proof, but our family... *all* our blood relatives anyway... well, we're wolf shifters."

I stared at him, waiting for the punchline. "I'm sorry, what?" I asked once he didn't elaborate. "I don't think I heard you right." I couldn't have. What he was saying made no sense.

And what a time to be making jokes!

Tommy stepped to the side, toward the large windows at the front of the house. "You don't need to be afraid, okay? When we're in shifter form, we are in complete control of our bodies. We aren't wild or feral, quite the opposite. We're still us, inside. You have to trust me on this."

I appreciated the change in topic, albeit strange as fuck, to free my mind of the fear Jamie had dredged up there, but I was kind of getting annoyed now. Whatever kind of joke or metaphor this was, I didn't get it, and I was emotionally spent.

I don't know how much more of this I can take.

"Um... I don't..."

"We wanted to show you and tell you earlier. We always wanted to be upfront, but your health was our main priority, whereas now... well, David went and lost control of his emotions and his inner wolf took over. So... he's right here."

I scoffed, my eyebrows crooked. "As a wolf, you mean?" That didn't make any sense. What was he playing at? And why?

"Ah... yeah," Tommy said, indicating to the foyer. "Literally."

I sat and stared with eyes as round as saucers, every ounce of logic in my mind trying to make sense of the impossibility that revealed itself to me.

A large, majestic gray wolf strolled into our dining room as if it owned the place and was completely at home.

"Oh my God!" I shrieked, jumping up and racing around the counter and into the kitchen. Which was a stupid mistake, really, because now I was trapped. "What the hell is that? Why is there a fucking wolf in the house, Tommy? Are you insane?"

The wolf sank down onto the floor, resting his head on his front paws while making a soft whining noise.

No. No, absolutely not. This isn't possible... he was joking. This is... Why? How? I—

My heart pounded like a tribal war drum, its strong, erratic beats like a chaotic melody in my ears. My vision dimmed at the edges, and I saw stars. I was feeling faint. My blood pressure had clearly skyrocketed, and I was about to be in serious trouble. "I... I can't breathe," I managed to gasp out as the world began to wobble.

Tommy ran for me, reaching me just in time and grabbing me as I staggered forward and fell into his arms. He carefully lay me down on the floor so I had no further to fall and couldn't hurt myself.

From where I lay on the warm wooden floorboards I watched in partial horror as the gray wolf became a man, a very naked man—one I recognized immediately. It was David,

He crawled toward me, his eyes stricken as he laid his hand on my head, running his fingers through my long hair. "It's okay, Stacey," he soothed. "I'm sorry. I'm so sorry I scared you. Please, please breathe."

Tommy disappeared from sight, no doubt going for his doctor's bag.

With no other choice available, I closed my eyes against the feeling that I needed to faint. Black spots burst at the corners of my eyes, and pain throbbed in my head, yet I couldn't deny what I saw. "You're a… a…" I stammered.

"A wolf, yes," David said. "I'm sorry, sweetheart, but it's genetic. We don't have any more choice on that one than anyone has in choosing their skin color. It's just how it is. I can't—*we* can't—change who we are."

Tommy returned and checked my blood pressure while listening to the baby's heartbeat with his stethoscope.

So many things suddenly made sense now. Words like "pack" and "mate", and a few of the odd smiles I'd seen on Nancy's and Lexie's faces, as though they'd been hiding a secret from me and were just waiting for me to discover the strange and seemingly impossible truth.

It was this. It was always this.

"We need to get her to the hospital," Tommy said firmly, pulling the stethoscope from his ears and the pressure band from my arm. "I'll call the ambulance."

"No!" I cried. "You can't! It's a public place. Jamie will get to me there, I know it. Please! Don't make me go." This time when David growled, I wasn't afraid.

He truly does love me and trust me, after all… "If he comes for you, he better be ready for a real fucking fight. It's been a while since our pack has had a good challenge, and I know my cousins would love to take that asshole down just as much as we do," he said.

I smiled a little and closed my eyes, willing my body to be calm. Jamie was a cunning bastard, and he had paid goons that fought his battles for him. But with *literal* wolves on my side, did I finally stand a chance?

Could I truly be free?

CHAPTER 17

DAVID

I'd never lost control of my wolf before or felt ashamed of myself… but as I paced the hospital hallway outside of Stacey's bedroom, I had to admit to being both and it smarted in a way I was distinctly uncomfortable with. When the door opened and my brother walked out a second later, I rushed over to him. "Is she okay?" I asked, the question rushing out of me in a *whoosh* along with the breath I'd been holding.

"At the moment," he said, his eyes shadowed with worry.

"And the baby?" I prompted, my heart racing.

Oh, my God. I'll never forgive myself if something happens to the baby.

"All good for now," he assured me. "I've called Dr. Morton and he'll be in this evening." Despite the reassuring news, Tommy's brow was furrowed, and his lips were pinched.

I crossed my arms over my chest defensively, my anxiety over our mate still unconvinced it could chill out just yet. "What aren't you telling me, brother?"

Tommy sighed. "I don't think she'll be allowed to come home again. After this episode, they'll want her on permanent, supervised bed rest, at least for the next few weeks. I had to put her in the Trendelenburg position because she started to cramp up and I was worried she was going into pre-term labor again."

"Holy fuck," I breathed as I pressed my fist to my mouth. I hadn't understood half of that, but it couldn't be good. Basically, my takeaway was that special precautions were being taken, which meant our mate was facing trouble. "Is there anything I can do?"

"Well, you could go in there and try and undo the fucking damage you caused by practically calling her a whore."

I blinked at him.

What the fuck is this, then?

"But I didn't..."

"You did!" my brother growled at me. "What would you call it? You basically said she got pregnant by her ex, then tried to fob the baby off on us. You implied she was some kind of cunning bitch, and you know that's the damn furthest thing from what she is! She's our damned sunshine, David."

My throat tightened and my wolf rose to the surface again, offering me respite from the emotions coursing through me. "I..."

Tommy pushed past me and headed off down the hall. "Just get in there and fix it. I'm not losing my mate because you couldn't keep your temper under control," he threw over his shoulder.

I inhaled sharply through my nose and pushed open the door to Stacey's private room.

She was lying down in her slightly inverted bed wearing a plain, open-backed hospital gown. Her eyes were filled with tears, and she was continually rubbing her belly in circles.

I wasn't sure if she was trying to calm herself down or the baby, but the frantic energy in the room was electric and not good for her. "How are you doing, sweetheart?" I asked, coughing to clear my throat.

"Um…" she mumbled as she gulped and looked up at the ceiling, avoiding my gaze.

I sat down in the chair opposite the bed, not wanting to upset her anymore than I already had. "I'm so sorry about wolfing out on you, Stacey. I didn't mean to, I swear. I haven't lost control like that in, well, *ever* actually."

Our parents had taught us early on how to control our shifter, and they were going to kick my ass when they found out what I'd done. I'd compromised our mate by losing control. A pregnant human woman did not need the added stress of discovering wolf shifters out of the blue for the first time when she was already in high-risk territory and had just discovered her ex-husband was stalking her.

She nodded and wiped at the tears on her cheeks, ever the trooper. "It's okay."

"No, it's not," I said, crushed by the pain she was so evidently experiencing—and it was all my fault, or at least, a good half of it. "Not what I did and not what I said. I'm really sorry." How did I explain that I was mortally ashamed of what I'd said and done? How could I convey in mere words that I no longer cared whose baby was in her belly. And all that mattered at all was that she was ours, no matter what.

"I'm grateful for one thing," she said, though her voice wavered with a note of uncertainty. "Tommy assured me that you guys are strong enough to stop Jamie if he tries to take me. He said you won't let it happen."

A growl rolled through my vocal cords which I quickly shook off, slapping my inner wolf down and asserting control. "Sorry. Yes, you're absolutely right. That asshole isn't getting within twenty feet of you ever again. We have your back, the entire family."

She nodded again, offering me a small smile, but she had shut down. She wasn't about to tell me anything. She was still hurting and not ready to let down her walls again any time soon.

I slid to the edge of my chair and leaned forward, resting my elbows on my knees, unwilling to let her lock herself down and shut us out entirely. "Stacey, tell me about your life before us. When did you get married?"

"Ah…" Stacey looked up again, blinking rapidly to clear her eyes of more tears. "You don't want to hear about my past," she said quietly.

"I do," I said. "It's my fault for not asking before. Tommy knew you'd been married, but I didn't. I should have laid down proper foundations for us. I should have learned everything there was to know about you. So, please? I want to know you. All of you. The light, the dark, and everything in between."

She sighed and shifted a little, making herself more comfortable before she spoke. "I filed for divorce a few weeks ago, now, through a lawyer back in California. I imagine he probably found me through all of that." She shook her head as if she should have known better than to flee a monster and leave behind a necessary paper trail.

I could feel the guilt and blame rolling over her. "He said he'd hire a private detective, if need be," I said, giving her whatever information I had gleaned from the asshole. "This isn't your fault. He's a punk and clearly, he was never going to let you get away without a fight. But you have us, now."

My mate gulped and sniffed, reaching for the Kleenex box. She looked so fragile and so beautiful, even in her compromised and delicate state.

"Tell me," I urged. "Anything at all that you think we should know. Tell me everything."

She blew her nose and heaved herself up to a higher sitting position, which was difficult given the angle of the thing. "Okay… but you aren't allowed to get mad, okay?"

I can't promise that.

But I had no choice. I wasn't going to get the truth out of her unless she trusted me and my word. "Go for it," I encouraged.

She stared down at her hands for a moment, then started talking. "I studied interior design, barely making ends meet on a scholarship, while also working full time. Both my parents are older, and they never put any money aside for my education. But despite that, I made it on my own. Unfortunately, I happened to meet Jamie one night during my final year. He was charming and had money, and he just kind of... sucked me into this vortex. He proposed after six months, and before I graduated he told me that he didn't want me to work because he could take care of me."

She stared down, the red blush of shame coloring her cheeks. "I know it sounds horrible and like a cop out, but after struggling with money my whole life it seemed nice to be looked after; to have someone that even wanted that kind of life for me."

I clenched my teeth so hard I heard them cracking inside my head. I knew what was coming next, but forced myself to nod. "Go on."

She shrugged, deflated by the haunting story of her past which was far too typical of many others I'd heard. "We got married and the day I signed that marriage license he immediately started wanting me to change. It was little things at first, like my hair and the way I dressed. Then he didn't want me going out so much, then he got rid of the cleaner and said it was my job now. To cook, to clean, to keep the house to the level he was accustomed to. And at first, I didn't mind, I really didn't. I wanted us to be happy. I wanted to do my part... but *nothing* I ever did was ever good enough. And I just," she sighed. "I can't explain it. It just all went to hell, and before I knew it I was trapped."

I got up and moved over to the seat next to the bed to close the distance between us, to offer her the security of my presence and strength. I didn't know a lot about controlling, manipulative men firsthand. My dad was a great man, as were most of the men in my pack. But Stacey wasn't lying, that was obvious. So, what had been the trigger point? "Tell me more. Why did you eventually leave?"

She stared at me, meeting my gaze with a fire I hadn't expected to see. "Because he told me that he was going on a business trip and that he'd planted cameras in our house so he could watch me while he was gone."

I groaned, appalled. "Are you fucking with me?"

What a fucking psycho, insecure dick.

She shook her head. "No. He always dropped little hints that he knew where I was. Or he'd call and tell me that he had people everywhere. He'd even introduce me to people, then tell me afterward they were hitmen. Men who specialized in making sure wives stayed loyal to their husbands."

She visibly shuddered. "The day he went on his business trip, despite the fear and the threat of hitmen, I ran away. I took some cash, and a few clothes, but that was it. And just so you know, we honestly hadn't had sex in months. *Months.* I didn't want to. I couldn't stand the thought of him touching me. I told him I had infections, made up excuses and just... you know... put him off."

"I believe you," I told her, because really, it didn't matter. And I had to extend my trust to her if I expected hers in return.

She blinked at me, her gaze searching. "You do?"

"Of course I do," I answered, reaching for her hand. "And it doesn't matter to me, anyway. This baby is *yours*, and I want *you*. We're a package deal, all of us—together—sweetheart."

Her eyes shimmered again with unshed tears, then she nodded. "You're right," she said, but then looked away.

I couldn't help but feel like I'd done or said the wrong thing.

Shit.

"I *do* believe you, Stacey. I just meant that the baby is obviously biologically Tommy's, and we've already made our own little family, haven't we? The three of us and our child—our daughter? I mean it doesn't matter to me that it's not *mine*... I'm here for you all, regardless."

She nodded, but she didn't say anything else and gently withdrew her hand from mine.

With every passing second of silence that eclipsed between us, I began to feel like I was intruding on her time. She didn't want me here anymore and I didn't know how to take back my words or reword them any better. I'd fucked up again even as I bloody well tried to fix it!

With a quiet groan Stacey slowly slid down the bed and lay on her side, her back to me.

I stood up, hands in my pockets, feeling like a boy in trouble. "Do you want me to go?" I asked.

"I might try to get some sleep," she answered simply, closing her eyes.

I glanced toward the door. Our town hospital was small, and there were no full-time security guards. So, there was no way I was going home if there was even a remote possibility that her ex-husband would show up. "I won't be far, okay?" I promised, leaning down to kiss her hair. "And I have my cell phone if you need me."

She didn't respond and it felt like a bucket of ice water on my soul. So, I left the room with my heart aching and my guilt heavier than ever.

Fuck me. How am I going to fix this?

CHAPTER 18

STACEY

My world had shrunk down to the sterile four white walls of my hospital room. The doctor informed me that I had no choice but to remain where I was until birth. My initial labor pains had stopped thanks to Tommy's quick thinking, but they hadn't ruled out putting me back into that stupid upside-down position if the contractions started again.

I felt broken and depressed, which I knew was terrible for the baby—*all that cortisol*—but I didn't know how to pull myself out of the deep sense of melancholy that plagued me like a shadow on my soul.

My baby deserves a better mother than me. I've made such a total mess of everything.

There was only one thing I felt I could be grateful for at this point, and that was that I was safe-ish. Tommy was always around, or Wade or Tanner. David too, of course. In fact, I was pretty sure that David was around all the time, though he steered clear of my room unless invited. But everyone else commented on seeing him. He seemed determined to make up for the fright he'd given me and the hurtful things he'd said by being on constant vigil.

Outside of the boys, I had a constant string of guests reminding me that someone was always just a call away. It was always nice seeing Nancy and Lexie. The 'human' women in the family. Some days I felt like I was surrounded by wolfy men, and the girls made me feel a little more grounded amid this storm of human and paranormal insanity in which I'd landed myself.

On the fifth day of my hospital stay, I was beginning to relax a little more. Our baby girl had officially reached thirty-one weeks and continued to grow stronger by the hour. A knock sounded on my door I called out to answer it, assuming it was Mary, the woman who brought me my dinner tray. It was five-thirty so everyone else had gone home for dinner.

"Come in!"

But the set of hard steel gray eyes that stared back at me the moment he stepped through the door sent a chill of immediate panic down my spine.

"Jamie," I whispered, frozen, the horror and fear of his presence kickstarting my heart into overdrive.

"Tsk, tsk, tsk," he admonished, shutting the door quietly behind him. "What are you doing here, wife? And with my baby too?"

I extended my arm in a flash and reached for my phone which lay within easy reach on the bedside table. I needed to send an *SOS* to the wolf family. They'd come. I knew it. They'd promised, every single one of them, to protect me.

But Jamie bolted forward, faster than me in my heavily pregnant state, and snatched the cell phone right out of my hand. "Oh no you don't." He slapped me on the hand like I was a mischievous child up to no good. It was almost darkly playful, but it stung from the impact and my skin went immediately red.

"What do you want?" I asked him, too afraid to ask him if

he'd received the divorce papers. He obviously had. Or he wouldn't be here.

He flicked back the bed covers without hesitation, as if that were still his right. "To take you home of course," he said. "Get up."

"I can't," I exclaimed, desperate and filled with anxiety over what this could mean for my baby, more than me. "I *need* to stay here. It's the doctor's orders!"

He grabbed my upper arm and gripped tightly. "Don't be ridiculous, dear. Now, get up. You're coming home with me."

"Ow, you're hurting me!" I cried, yanked physically out of bed by his iron grip and away from safety. My heart hammered in my chest and a brutal wave of wooziness slammed over me, triggered by the too fast movement. "Jamie... *please.*"

"No!" he snapped, glaring down at me. "You don't get to beg me to be nice here, Stace. You did the wrong thing, not me. You took my baby away, and you'll come home with me now."

Panic hit me hard and fast the further from safety I was pulled. I had to find a way to make him reject me, to leave me. I had to wound his pride and there was only one way to do that.

Surely, the truth will save me.

"It's not your baby!" I cried. "You *have* to realize that, Jamie. We hadn't slept together in months before I left."

He slapped me hard across the face with his spare hand, luckily his non-dominant or I would have been seeing stars.

I fell backward in pain, shocked by the unexpected blow. But he maintained an unforgiving hold on my arm, so I didn't fall far. "You're *mine*," he hissed. "Which makes that baby fucking mine. Got it?"

I whimpered in pain but couldn't find the will to respond, my head was reeling from the first physical attack he'd ever launched on me. He'd always been controlling, manipulative, and domineering, but he'd stopped short of physical violence. Apparently, it wasn't beyond him, anymore.

"Get dressed. Now," he snapped, his temper getting the better of him the longer I caused a delay on his plans.

"Okay," I whispered, blinking rapidly against the pain in my face making my eye feel like it was going to explode in my skull. "My clothes are in the drawers."

Jamie finally let go of my arm.

I gasped from the pain that flooded into my flesh the moment he released his death grip.

He pulled open the drawer roughly, grabbed all my clothes and dumped them on top of the bed. "Hurry up."

I nodded and swallowed back the tears in my throat that threatened to reveal just how close I was to breaking down. Jamie hated tears and he'd double down on me if he saw them. Luckily for me, I already had some underwear on but was forced to sit down and wriggle on some leggings, before attempting to struggle my way into a maternity top.

Jamie was watching me like a hawk with a keen eye trained on his prey.

I turned my back on him to pull on my oversized top, not wanting to allow him the privilege of seeing what was no longer his.

"I've seen it all before Stace. I've kept you naked a lot in the past, or have you already forgotten?"

I tried to hide my shudder as the memories returned, and the body shaming I'd endured as a result of being with a man who was never happy with anything short of perfection. But I kept it all inside, and as I dressed, I answered him simply. "Okay."

Without warning or expectation, a strange sort of calm settled upon me, though I wasn't sure why or even how. But all I knew with complete clarity was that I had to survive whatever was coming next. Not for my own sake, but for my daughter's. I'd gotten away from him once before, and I could do it again. I'd find a way to do it while she was still little, so that she'd have no memory of him. I would protect her from those scars no matter what it took; no matter what I had to personally sacrifice.

I didn't grab anything else from the room, though it broke my heart to do so. I left behind the pink blankets Nancy had bought for me, as well as the baby clothes in the top-drawer Tommy had dropped off just yesterday. I'd planned to give birth here and to hold my daughter for the very first time in my arms. I couldn't bear to disturb that vision in my mind, so I left it untouched, like a beautiful, untarnished memory of what could have been.

"Let's go," he said, almost urgently. "You're taking too long."

Is he worrying that one of my new wolf family will show up for me?

"Okay," I said again, staying as calm as I could force myself to be.

Jamie opened the door and pulled me out into the brightly lit hall, one hand on my arm, the other firmly at the small of my back.

I shuffled along, my body literally screaming at me to lie down again, to take the load off my feet. My back ached with every step and my belly felt too heavy now. But I kept moving without complaint, knowing that this entire situation was a marathon and I needed to pace myself if I was going to survive it.

"Hurry up," he said, pressing his hand more aggressively against my lower back and pushing me along.

I stumbled and almost fell, catching myself just in time. "I'm moving as fast as I can," I hissed at him, grabbing my huge belly to accentuate my issue. I'd likely pay for showing him outright aggression and attitude like that, but it couldn't be avoided.

Jamie looked me over with more scrutiny and seemed to wrap his head around the problem. Since he couldn't carry me out of the hospital without raising suspicion from the medical staff, he just set his jaw and continued to guide me onward.

Though he couldn't know it, I took my time as much as I dared. I could have managed to hurry more, but I wouldn't give him the satisfaction of running to his car, as though he was some kind of hero rescuing me. He was kidnapping me against my will. He was the damn villain, so I would make this as hard as I could for him without arousing his ire any further.

Ursula, a nurse who was good friends with Tommy, walked toward me, her brow furrowed. She knew what was going on with me as far as mine and the baby's health went.

She'll realize something is up. She'll raise the alarm with the boys.

I shook my head at her, only ever so slightly, but she got the move.

"You shouldn't be out of bed, Stacey," she said, shaking her head at me.

Jamie grabbed my hand, hard, willing me not to break character. "We're just going for a short walk," he explained with a forced smile that made me sick to my stomach. "We won't be long."

I gave Ursula a pointed look and a grimace. "Won't be long," I repeated with a strained smile and continued to shuffle along the hallway.

"Hurry up!" Jamie hissed at me again, his anger rising to the surface once more.

Surely, he won't slap or hurt me in public?

Like the sound of angelic trumpets signifying the arrival of Heaven's cavalry to the rescue, an unholy growl filled the air around us.

I closed my eyes on a sob, the sweet taste of relief overwhelming my senses.

I'm saved. Thank God.

"What the hell is that?" Jamie spat.

I stopped in my tracks and turned around, looking back the way Ursula had gone.

David was standing in the center of hallway, his hands tightened into fists, the wrath of Hell itself blazing in his beautiful eyes.

Jamie grabbed me, no doubt intending to use me a human meat shield, but I wasn't about to let him use me to get away from David. He deserved everything that was coming to him.

I stumbled on purpose and went down to the ground, careful of my belly, but using the fact that there was *no way* Jamie could drag me or carry me out of here successfully if I made it difficult for him.

David charged like a bull at a red flag, barreling straight into Jamie, and knocking him to the ground. Kneeling astride his chest, he punched him in the face over and over in a dizzying frenzy of righteous anger. "She's ours," David growled through clenched teeth. "That baby is ours. *She* is ours. You need to fucking leave her alone!"

I stared at my hero with my mouth agape. Jamie's face was bloodied and broken, and it was clear David had no intention of stopping. And yet, I couldn't find the words to make him stop. I almost didn't want to stop him.

Luckily for Jamie, Tommy and his cousins came running down the hall, and soon pulled David off.

"He's had enough!" warned Tanner.

"Come on, David," Wade urged.

The cousins dragged him away, denying him the pleasure of direct contact any longer.

Meanwhile Tommy assessed Jamie's health. He might hate my ex just as much as I did, but he was a doctor first and foremost and he would not dishonor the Hypocritic Oath.

Swallowing hard, I had to look away from my abuser's

broken face. There was just so much blood. He was practically unrecognizable.

"Get off me!" David growled, shoving off his cousins to rush over to me. He dropped to his knees at my feet, his heart in his throat and his gaze plaintive and hopeful. "Sweetheart, are you okay? Will you ever forgive me?"

Without a single heartbeat's hesitation, I threw myself into David's waiting arms and cried, longer and harder than I ever had in my whole life. The nightmare was finally over.

CHAPTER 19

DAVID

My poor, beautiful woman was sobbing like her heart was broken and crashing down all around her.

So, I just held her, calming her down as best I could. I gently stroked her hair and rubbed her belly and promised her that everything was going to be okay now. I'd personally file charges against that mother fucker, and I'd burn his house down, too. He was *never* getting anywhere near my woman again.

The police were called, and Jamie was dragged away for surgery to try and fix the damage I'd done.

I hope I fucked his face for life. Asshole, pretty boy.

I carried my pregnant mate back to her bed to be checked over by the staff and I refused to leave her side, even when Tommy asked me to. "No." I snapped at him. "I've been keeping my distance and look what happened! No, means *no*, brother. I'm not leaving her. Never again."

Stacey smiled at me with tears in her eyes, clearly overwhelmed but grateful for my protective and possessive brand of support during this frightening and trying time for her.

I held her hand as they poked and prodded at her and declared she still very much needed to remain on bed rest. When everyone left, including Tommy, I finally melted onto the bed with her, dropping my head and pressing a kiss to her swollen belly. "Please forgive me, Stacey."

She stroked my head and ran her fingers through my hair, seemingly willing me to feel comforted, when it was her who needed it most.

"I should have always trusted you," I lamented. "And I'm so sorry I made you feel like I didn't want you or the baby. I was acting like a jealous ass. I'm better than that, I promise."

"It's okay," she finally said after a time. "I understand why you felt the way you did, and it's okay that you were worried. It's a very human thing to feel. And I'm happy to do a paternity test to prove to you she's Tommy's. I've already asked the nurse and she said we can do that as soon as she's born."

I kissed her belly again and shook my head. "No, that's not necessary. She's ours and I love her already." Flooded with emotions I'd never felt before, I lifted my head and stared at my mate. "And I love you, Stacey, so much. I thought I was going to die when I saw him with you, trying to take you away. It was like having my heart torn out of my chest."

She huffed out a laugh. "I almost died on the spot when he walked back into my life, at your house, and here, again. But I'm okay. I promise. I've learned that I'm a little tougher than I ever thought I was." And she looked it, in fact, she had more color in her cheeks than she'd had all week. The rosiness suited her.

I tilted my head at her, a silly wolfy mannerism, and assessed the feelings emanating from her. "If you don't mind my saying, you seem... content in a strange way."

Stacey actually smiled at me this time. "Is it terrible that I feel, relieved?" she asked.

"Not at all. Jamie won't be bothering you again, I promise."

She squeezed my hand and settled into the bed. "I know and it's all thanks to you." She closed her eyes and sighed. "I might need to rest for a while, I'm exhausted, but can you stay, please?"

I kissed the top of her head. "I'm not going anywhere, sweetheart."

And I wasn't. I'd hired a new chef during the week—an old friend from culinary school. Before Stacey I'd never imagined I could let someone else run my restaurant, my kitchen, or my business. But she'd very quickly shown me what my true priorities were. Nothing mattered in life if I didn't have my mate or my child. Their well-being and happiness was everything to me. And no amount of money or success, or control over my work life, was ever going to make me as truly happy as this spectacular woman.

She murmured something that I didn't quite catch as she drifted off to sleep, interrupting my train of thought.

I leaned forward. "Sorry, what was that, beautiful?" I whispered.

"I love you too, David," she whispered back.

My heart broke and was remade in that moment and I knew my life—*our* life—was never going to be the same again.

THE NEXT SIX weeks were insanely busy. Stacey, of course, stayed in the hospital and we got an extra bed added to the room so that Tommy and I could stay with her as frequently as possible.

At thirty-seven weeks pregnant, Dr. Morton told us the baby and Stacey had waited long enough given the touch and go nature of their situation, and it was time for a C-section. There were tears of fear from Stacey—it certainly wasn't the dream birth she'd hoped for—but in the end, everything went well, and our beautiful daughter was born.

Margaret Rose Bailey. 6 lbs. 6 oz. and absolutely perfect.

Stacey and the baby stayed in the hospital for a few more days. Observation was required for the baby and Stacey needed medication after her surgery, then it was time to take her home.

Home.

I don't think I'd ever appreciated the word as much as I did, now. "Are you ready to go?" I asked.

Stacey was busy looking through the cupboard and the drawers for the sixth time to make sure she had everything.

Our sweet little Maggie was fast asleep in my arms and my heart beat with a steady, happy rhythm in my chest. I'd never known love like this before setting my eyes on my daughter. She was a perfect, mini replication of her mother, with her perfect Cupid's Bow lips and a cute tuft of downy blonde hair.

"Yeah, I think so," she said, grabbing the baby bag.

Tommy wheeled an extra suitcase we'd needed to pack everything out of the room and offered me a brotherly nod.

"It's strange... this has been home for so long," Stacey said, glancing back.

I put my arm around my brave, beautiful woman. "Let's go home, for real."

We had a surprise for Stacey, and I couldn't wait to show her. We took the baby to the car, the new family SUV that Tommy had bought, and jumped in. Me in the passenger seat, Tommy driving, and Stacey in the back with the baby.

"You ready to see your new house?" I asked, grinning at our mate as I turned around in my seat.

Tommy started the car and drove toward Nancy's, Wade's, and Tanner's place.

Stacey frowned at me in confusion. "Um, what new house?"

"You'll see," I said and turned back around to face the front.

"You guys bought a new house, and you didn't tell me?" she asked, sounding shocked.

I shrugged. "If you don't like it, we'll buy another."

And we would. There was always a need for good rentals in an area like this and if she didn't want this home, we'd find a way to make her happy. That was our new goal in life, after all. The happiness of our girls, our family.

We turned into our new street and drove past our cousins' place.

"Hey! That's Nancy's house," Stacey said, excitement clear in her sweet voice.

Tommy pulled into our new driveway. "And this is our new home. We thought that you'd want to be near Nancy, and this place has five bedrooms. It needs a lot of design work and renovations done, but we figured, you'd want to do all of that. It might even be a bit of fun, a project to attack bit by bit as the baby grows."

We got out of the car, and I scooped Maggie up out of her car seat and wrapped her in a blanket. "Come on, baby. Let's show Mommy the new house."

Tommy took Stacey to the front door and handed her the keys with a grin on his face. "We haven't even opened it up yet, we've been waiting for you."

There were tears in our mate's eyes as she beheld the home we'd chosen for her. "Guys, this is too much."

I laughed. "No, it's not. But I'm afraid we can't stay here tonight because it's not ready. We still have the town house, of course, though, and we can move in here as soon as you're happy with it."

Stacey wiped away the few tears that spilled down her cheeks, slid the key into the lock, and opened the grand front door.

Tommy grabbed her up in his arms and carried her over the threshold.

Stacey squealed in delight, her eyes wide. This was her

happily ever after movie moment and she deserved to revel in every second of it.

Tommy finally put her down in the large formal living room and stepped back to allow her to drink it all in.

She turned in a slow circle, her expression one of awe. "Oh my," She whispered as she walked around the room, staring at the forest green walls and crown moldings. "It's *so* beautiful. There is definitely a lot to work with here."

Tommy and I shared a knowing grin. "We've been hoping you'd like it."

She nodded and made ridiculously cute happy noises. "I can't believe you actually bought this for us!"

"Come upstairs," Tommy said, taking her hand and leading her up the double stairwell. "It's structurally sound, of course, we had the engineers in to check on everything before we bought it. But I think you'll need to use your interior design skills on every room because everything's very outdated. The bathrooms are pink. The kitchen is green..."

Their voices faded off as they went down the hallway upstairs to investigate the bedroom situation and no doubt discuss Stacey's interior design opinions. The master bedroom here was small, but the engineers had already said we could safely knock down a wall into the second bedroom and make a huge master to cater to our needs as a throuple.

"Let's leave them to it and go see the backyard," I told Maggie, making sure her blanket was wrapped tightly around her. She was sleeping in my arms peacefully, oblivious to everything going on around her. I'd never seen a child look more like an angel than my own daughter. She was what dreams were made of.

I walked her into the huge, presently ugly kitchen and opened the back door. There, on the broken patio, I sat down with Maggie and looked out over the yard as I told her stories of all the things we were going to do together once we settled in. I was going to get her a swimming pool, string up a tree swing, and we'd have parties all year round—just because. I'd get our handy cousins to build her a tree house to climb, and an amazing sand pit to play in too.

She'd be surrounded by cousins her own age, and have a huge, protective wolfy family of shifters there for her every step of the way. Our beautiful Margaret Rose would grow up knowing she was loved beyond measure. No matter what life threw at us now; we were ready for it and the worst of it was behind us. As a pack, we were strong, and Stacey and Maggie were its newest members.

With my heart full, I gazed up into the clear blue sky and offered a prayer of thanks to the universe.

For my mate. For my daughter. For my heart. For our impossibly perfect pairs happily ever after... Thank you.

EPILOGUE

STACEY

Three months later

Our home came together so much faster than I'd even dared hope for. My vision for the house was simple, classic, and timeless, but with lots of functional storage and 'homey' vibes so that everyone who walked in our front door would immediately feel a sense of peace, welcome, and comfort.

David and Tommy knew *everyone* in town between them, so once I had my designs in order, the tradesmen arrived in literal droves. Painters, cabin makers, carpenters, plumbers, electricians, and carpeting experts. The lot!

In no time flat, our incredible, double-story, period home was done, and the big day had arrived. We were moving in tomorrow!

"I can't believe we're finally going to be living in our house!" I said over a dinner of scrumptious take away surrounded by a sea of packing boxes.

"It's going to be great," Tommy reassured me.

"I hope Maggie's okay tonight," I said, ever the fretful mother, glancing at her packed-up room.

"She'll be fine sweetheart, it's only for twenty-four hours," David reminded me.

I nodded and twirled my spaghetti with my fork. David and Tommy's parents had been amazing with their granddaughter *and* with me. I'd pumped enough milk to feed Maggie for a full day, and they were happily babysitting while we made the move.

It was a beautiful gesture, because it meant I would get a full night's sleep tonight, and we could focus on getting the house set up for her tomorrow. The movers were coming in the morning, and I was hoping that if nothing else, our bedrooms would be set up at the new house by tomorrow night. We could take our time setting up everything else afterward.

"Are we getting an early night?" David asked, going to grab the chocolate mousse containers from the kitchen. "I don't want to hurt your feelings, but you look pretty tired, babe. We've been going non-stop..."

I didn't take the comment as a rejection or insult. It was true. I *was* tired, but I wanted my men, so much. It had been way too long.

Between a few complications that arose due to the C-section and an adorable baby who refused to sleep more than a few hours at any given time, I literally hadn't had sex with them in months! And I was craving their touch like never before.

Not that they weren't affectionate, they were amazing. I had no complaints. They were amazing partners and fathers... but I needed more.

I need my lovers.

"Yeah, an early night would be good," I said, taking a spoon and dipping it into the luxurious chocolatey dessert. "But not to sleep."

Tommy froze mid move, he'd been clearing the table and he

stopped, one plate hilariously still in the air. "Ah... what do you mean?" he asked.

I slid my gaze his way and gave him a cheeky grin. "I mean, I'm *all* healed up and I was hoping my men would make love to me tonight."

Without any secrets between us. No boundaries. No issues. I'd never been happier, and according to everyone who knew them, they were too.

"You want to..."

I nodded and grabbed the chocolate mousse off David, because he was sitting there like a stunned mullet too. I ate some more, enjoying the rich decadence. I'd put a lot of my weight back on since the birth, but my men seemed to genuinely love it. They loved me no matter what, but they were big fans of my curves, apparently!

David's eyes flared. "Bed. Now." He held out his hand.

"Right now?" I grabbed his hand, but clung tight to my dessert. "The chocolate mousse..."

"Bring it with you," he said with a growl.

A shiver of anticipation thrilled through me, and I squealed as he practically ran me to our bedroom, with Tommy hot on our heels.

"You sure about this?' David asked, his chest rising and falling fast. "Are you okay?"

I nodded with a grin, allaying their fears. "Absolutely. Please! I miss you guys so much. I can't bear to wait any longer."

David began to strip off, as did Tommy.

I walked casually to the bed and sat down, savoring my chocolate, licking it from the spoon as I watched my men get naked.

Damn, they're beautiful.

David was all rippling hard muscle and strength, while Tommy was bigger and broader, but every bit just as beautiful.

I licked the last of the confection from my spoon, set them aside, and dropped to my knees on the soft carpet before them. "I want to suck both of you." I told them, and it wasn't a request.

With a shared smirk of their impending pleasure, they stepped up to me, side by side, their cocks already hardening at my proposition.

I reached up and wrapped both of their shafts in my hands, squeezing my palms around their warm flesh.

Their combined groans filled the air like a carnal song.

I smiled with feminine satisfaction as I leaned forward and kissed them both, one at a time. I licked the heads, swirling my tongue around them, then sucked them deep into my mouth. They were both salty and perfect against the sweetness of my tongue. I took my time, moving between them both, drawing out their ecstasy until I felt my own wetness dampening my panties.

David finally growled and pulled me to my feet. "You need to get naked, sweetheart, or I'm going to rip those clothes right off this gorgeous body of yours."

I squeaked with delight as I helped them take off my clothes, lifting my arms above my head to remove my top. I absolutely loved the new leggings I was wearing. So, I didn't want them ripped off me, and I didn't doubt for a second that David would make good on his threat. With a quick wiggle and shake, I slid out of them and tossed them to the side out of harm's way.

Then they were on me like wolves on a delectable feast.

David kissed my lips with the urgency of a starving man, his tongue seeking out mine with a fervor that took my breath away.

Meanwhile Tommy's mouth was at my neck, peppering my flesh with kisses and nipping it between his teeth as his hands gripped my waist.

They'd missed me like I'd missed them. It was finally clear to me. They'd been patiently waiting, not complaining, and just biding their time until I gave them the green light. No matter how much they'd yearned for me, they'd respected my healing body and valued my consent and choice above all else.

I kissed David back with all the passion in my soul, eager to show him that I was as keen to be claimed as he was to claim. His fingers slipped between my thighs, making me gasp and cry out against his lips. Not wanting to ignore my beautiful other mate, I turned my head and captured Tommy's mouth with my own.

David relentlessly stroked my clit, teasing me toward release with every move.

Tommy pinched, caressed, and tweaked my nipples, causing me to yelp against his lips and jump in their combined embrace.

They played my body like musicians play their instrument—beautifully, almost religiously, and with heart wrenching passion. We made music with our bodies, every strangled breath a note in an orchestral masterpiece of our own making.

My hands were everywhere on them that I could possibly reach; their gorgeous faces, strong muscles, and throbbing, rock-hard cocks. It was everything I'd waited for. But when Tommy finally groaned and moved us toward the bed, I couldn't have been happier to know that relief and unbridled bliss was in sight.

He lay down on his back on the bed and gestured to me to join him. "Climb on top, sweetheart."

I did so with glee, throwing my leg over his waist and sliding over his belly. His hard cock pressed against my ass at first, so I pushed up and tilted my hips back, opening my pussy for him. When his head slid along my wetness I pressed down, guiding him inside of me. I gasped at that first feeling of connection between us as he forged inside of me.

He grabbed my breasts, squeezing and manipulating them, before grazing my agonizingly pert nipples.

I arched my back as inch by inch I took him inside of me. My body felt different than it even had before, but it was still perfect.

My body might have changed, but it had given life and now it was time to give and receive pleasure.

David stepped up behind me and pressed on my lower back. "Can you lean forward for me, sweetheart?"

I did as instructed, more than willing to go with the flow as I lowered myself down to kiss Tommy. As soon as our lips met, I felt something I'd never experienced before, and my body seized, tightening in response.

David's fingers were on my ass, running cold lube over my virgin hole.

A wave of fear washed over me at the unknown, but I didn't question it.

This was what I'm meant for, isn't it? Two men. My men.

I moaned with abandon as Tommy shifted underneath me, gently thrusting up into me. My body was taught and strung out, needing the release that only my men, my mates, could give me.

"I'll go slow, okay?" David whispered into my ear.

I simply nodded, focusing on kissing Tommy.

The larger of the two brothers moved a hand between us and started gently fingering my clit.

Sensations exploded inside of me, and I gasped as my pussy clamped down around his cock as the first wave of my release floored me.

David's cock butted up against my asshole, easing inside of me too slowly as he groaned.

Desperate to be done with the new feeling, I pushed back and he slid inside of me all at once. I gasped out at the strange pain that threatened to overwhelm me and shuddered as the ecstasy of my orgasm warred with the discomfort assaulting me from behind.

Tommy pressed on my clit with greater fervor and began to thrust up inside of me again, the pleasure of his movements distracted and calmed me instantly.

David hadn't dared to move again after hearing me cry out. He was waiting for me to adjust and give him that all-important green light.

But I needed more. I pressed back against him, and he slid in deeper and deeper, until I felt like I couldn't take it a moment more. Both of my mates were completely buried inside me. We couldn't be anymore connected than this. "Move," I gasped out, my whole body shivering with the tension of being so, so incredibly full. "Keep going! Please. Yes!"

David thrust in and out of me, utilizing short, swift moves that filled me with desperation, his sac slapping against my pussy in the most erotic way imaginable.

Beneath me, Tommy started to fuck me in earnest, thrusting up with his hips, he sunk himself into the hilt, his hands firm on my waist.

They shattered my world, moving together like a well-oiled machine.

No, like a perfect pair.

I was caught in the middle of a storm of sensation. My body was on fire and my breath came in helpless, labored pants. My belly seized faster than I could have ever imagined possible, and my orgasm exploded inside me. My pussy tightened around Tommy's cock and my ass gripped David's, making them both to growl as I shook and spasmed between them like a livewire thrashing with electricity on the street.

I'd never felt anything like it. It swallowed me alive and dragged me under into a world of rapture and never-ending bliss. Squeezing my eyes closed, there was no way I could prevent or contain the screams that tore my throat as I came again, and again. Unable to stop the rolling pleasure, I had no choice but to ride and endure the wave as it just slammed into me repeatedly like a truck on rewind.

I held onto my men for dear life, as they fucked me harder and faster.

Then David began to curse aloud, his movements becoming jerky and erratic as he lost control of his body.

I reached for him, relying on Tommy's grasp of my waist. David's hands were on my hips, so I grabbed his arm as his hoarse, animalistic cry rang throughout the room. He filled me with his hot seed moments before Tommy followed.

We collapsed into a pile of sweaty bodies and kissed one another.

My belly and pussy continued to shudder after the most Earth-shattering orgasms of my life, like aftershocks in the wake of a quake. Breathlessly, I whispered to my men how incredible this was and how grateful I was to be theirs. "I love you, Tommy. I love you, David," I sighed. "Thank you for everything."

I don't think I've ever been happier. I've got everything I've ever wanted and more.

The thought blew my mind. And with my last conscious thought spent, my wolves wrapped me up in the strength and in a tangle of limbs we succumbed to sleep and dreams. And in the morning, when the sun rose, we'd wake to start our new life— together.

THE END

www.ingramcontent.com/pod-product-compliance
Lightning Source LLC
Chambersburg PA
CBHW071818190726
48292CB00005B/1508